LEE'S GHOST

LEE'S GHOST

Petronella Pulsford

Constable · London

First published in Great Britain 1990
by Constable and Company Limited
10 Orange Street London WC2H 7EG
Copyright © 1990 Petronella Pulsford
Set in Linotron Palatino 11pt by
CentraCet, Cambridge
Printed in Great Britain by
St Edmundsbury Press Ltd
Bury St Edmunds, Suffolk

A CIP catalogue record for this book
is available from the British Library

ISBN 0 09 469850 3

To Mary

Prologue

Lee sat on her double bed and stared down through the window into the light-lozenge of the bar across the road. The window she looked through was framed on either side by floor-length, deep-brown velvet curtains one of which she stroked, taming herself, with her right hand as she gazed.

Outside the wind was playing like an excited infant with pieces of newspaper in the gutter. The paper formed itself into cartoon-like ghost-figures in the darkness. Somebody in a house opposite came out into the hallway and abruptly closed the front door, sealing in the amber warmth. Somewhere a child was shouting, for justice it seemed.

Lee could see Gabriel in profile. He had a pint of beer in front of him and was talking to the small, Welsh publican. When he had finished speaking he laughed. Lee felt as if she were watching a television through a shop window. Gabriel's broad, thick lips spread wide apart and upwards and downwards and turned his face into a maze of rubber inroads. I am making a laugh, the face said. I am making a laugh. His hair looks like the bonnet of a taxi-cab, Lee thought, sleeked back like that. Suddenly he looked up at her window. Her body jerked. His face had straightened out and he looked worried.

Such severance, Lee thought, such a jolt. The needle

has been lifted before the music ended. I don't care about his worry. Oh, but I do. This record has got to finish playing, some time. She kneeled swiftly up on the bed and pulled the velvet hangings to shut out the scene.

When Gabriel and Lee had together inhabited her strange new home of muted greens and beiges and lemon-coloured walls and black beams and rich, red rugs and rocking-chairs and pinewood tables and wood-framed mirrors and flowers and Casa Pupo rugs and Japanese lanterns, their life had had the ambience of a circus in the air, silken-canopied and vibrant, unsupported but strong, both unique and popular, both miraculous and cheap: a brilliant entertainment touched occasionally with terror. They had lived like high-fliers in the '20s, cocktail-happy but with a child's belief in eternal, familial security. The world had been their darling pet, everybody their concern, and when ugliness struck they had simply retired to their castle to breathe the ambrosia of the gods.

But the cocktail became poisonous to Lee and ugliness seemed to threaten her more often and one day she found herself suffering from a delusion that her blood was turning black. I need a safety net up here, she thought, but there was none. Suddenly she was clinging as if in fear of falling or drowning and she had forgotten how to walk the tightrope, she had forgotten how to fly on the trapeze, she had forgotten how to don her clown's make-up and how to lead her proud team of stallions. She found herself with no resources, no alternatives. Gabriel's and Lee's paradise had become a concentration camp and Lee had lost touch with everything else and found herself terrified of what lay beyond its walls.

She heard the creak as the door to the bedroom started to open slowly and she looked around and up,

8

conditioned, expecting to see him standing there, hair bristling like a skinhead's, eyes round and lit up as they were when he'd been doing tough, physical work. But it was Hosanna, her cat, who came nuzzling through and stood, white legs bent, blinking at his mistress in the stream of light from the passage.

'Hosanna.' She reached down and picked him up and held him close, wondering as usual at the softness, the flexibility, the resilience in him that defied ownership and control, that simply shone, existed, throbbed, flew. Gabriel was still there with them. His body was in the building across the way but his soul was still there with them.

Hosanna licked her nose. The doorbell rang. Petals fell from the Michaelmas daisies on the bedside table. Lee felt as if she had been wakened from a deep sleep by an ugly and unwanted alarm-clock. She bared her teeth at Hosanna and growled. He nestled deeper into the hollow of her shoulder. 'Go,' she said to him as she put him down. I must relax, be nice, she thought. Instead of Gabriel, she visualized a slender, flowing river transporting lilies and translucent bodies undershadowed by fleeting fish. The doorbell rang again.

As she walked down the stairs with Hosanna behind her Lee wondered whether she had been possessed. She debated whether relationships might have souls like people that existed before conception and after death. Or perhaps Gabriel is having his revenge, she pondered. She remembered a story about an early poltergeist investigator directing questions via a medium to a spirit that had caused violent disturbances in a house in Paris, smashing all the windows and forcing the inhabitants to leave. The spirit explained that he had been a rag and bone man who had died fifty years ago in the same area and that he resented people because they had mocked him during his lifetime. He had obtained the energy to cause the disturbances from a maidservant in the house who was unaware that she was being used. Or perhaps I just love Gabriel and can't let go of him, Lee thought as she reached the front door.

Her caller was a man of about her height. He wore thin-rimmed glasses and one of his ears was swollen around the lobe as if he had been a boxer. He was about fifty, Lee estimated. His skin was sallow and thick like the skin of a faded and slightly moistened pomegranate. She noticed that his trousers were short and rode about two inches above his ankles. He carried a pair of new-looking black leather gloves in his hands and was wringing them as if testing them for texture. His eyes were dark and one eyebrow was absent while the other was fully formed, dark and reached the bridge of his nose. This abnormality gave his face the look of a formidable book with its front cover missing. When he spoke it was with a French accent.

'I have been informed that you have a room for lodgings,' he said, his eyes looking at her but turned somehow downwards and inwards away from her. 'I am alone now for my father has passed and I am searching for habitation.'

He is lying, Lee thought. Something wrong, something Mephistophelian, something subterranean, something sent here, not belonging.

'Ah. I see,' she said. 'I am so sorry.'

She wanted to turn him away immediately but felt that this would be too harsh. He was out of the question, of course, as a lodger but there was a part of her, a new part she thought, to which he appealed. On one level he came across as a sort of brain-damaged pugilist with the soul of a Maurice Chevalier. On another . . .

10

Lee felt a shock pass through her again as when Gabriel had turned to look at her. He brings something in with him, she thought. She hesitated and as she did so saw Gabriel lumbering down the hill on the pavement opposite. Just seeing his back in the night light weakened her defences so that she could feel his personality flooding her. She raised her left hand to grasp the back of her neck. In her own grip she said:

'Do come in. It is so cold tonight.' Although the air felt fairly warm around them.

After she had closed the front door she posed against it for a moment with one hand behind her against the rough wood and the other on her chest, still, commanding and two-dimensional like a female lead in a '40s film. Lauren Bacall had been making an exit on her famous line, Lee remembered. I am becoming ridiculous. This unwelcome, yet unavoidable new character has robbed me of my authenticity.

'I am called Louis,' the man said, and placed his gloves on the seat of her rocking-chair. It tilted slightly and one of the gloves fell to the floor. It looked like a dead animal amid the floral patterns. Hosanna leapt into the air and landed by it.

'She is an acrobat,' said Louis as the cat smelled the glove and pawed it gently, trying to bring it to life. They stayed quiet for a while watching the cat until he gave up and curled himself away under the rocking-chair.

'It's a he,' Lee said.

'In France we had three cats,' he replied. 'Three generations. The children were cruel. They liked to frighten the youngest until she clung, whimpering. Is it correct, whimpering? *Les enfants* . . . One day my pipe was – they broke it. For malice.'

'Ah. A victim,' she thought. No, a malefactor. Projecting it.

11

'Will you sit down?' she offered. He chose to sit in a striped deckchair that had been put there for fun. Gabriel had brought it back for her on one of his marauding expeditions. Louis looked like a seaside joke and Lee laughed but then was sorry because he had gone into himself again.

'Your ceiling is cracked,' he said without looking up at it.

You're cracked, she suddenly, insanely, wanted to reply.

'I really am only wanting to let on a temporary basis,' she said instead. 'The bed in the room upstairs is large and there is a Casa Pupo rug – have you heard of Casa Pupo? This is a rather beautiful rug. It has a bone-white base and a black fringe all round and very subtle brown and beige markings. Light from the streetlamps comes in at night so the curtaining is heavy in that room. The wardrobes are in-built. Do you understand in-built? The walls are yellow. I suppose that a room is its atmosphere really. But, you see, I really am only wanting to let on a temporary basis.'

Gabriel's and my bedroom, she thought. How he hated it when we made love before getting into bed. It perplexed me, his need to do things properly and by the book when he was, after all, only a drunken sailor. On ships, of course, everything is shipshape. You pull your rope and I'll pull mine and bunks are for lights-out and no hanky-panky. He was locked away in a padded cell once, so he said. Perhaps he always feared being put away again. Gentle Gabriel, giant Gabriel, clown Gabriel, fascist puppeteer Gabriel, anarchist Gabriel, lover Gabriel.

'Would you like a brioche?' she asked. 'Oddly enough, I bought some brioches yesterday.'

'I have been to McDonalds,' replied Louis and started to rub his groin, to her horror until she saw that it was

12

a lifeless gesture, as erotic, as threatening, as smoothing out a crumpled cushion. Less so. She wished now that she had not let him in.

He was reaching out a hand and picking up a newspaper from the top of the Edwardian bookcase against the wall.

'You read the newspaper from a week ago,' he remarked, looking at the date and rocking gently.

'Oh, yes, I always do. I buy them and save them up to read a week later. I like being a week behind. I hate to know things instantaneously. I like to make my own timing. When I am really free I can read the newspaper a week late and believe that I am reading it a week early. Then things are my own truth.'

I feel accountable to this demon, she thought. Why? She was remembering a Guy Fawkes that Gabriel and she had made for the sad child in the betting shop down the hill. They had created a face for it out of red pepper slices and pieces of potato, and given it olives for eyes, and she had been unable to make love while it was in the bedroom, sitting happily in the corner, squinting at them. Gabriel had enjoyed her feyness and settled the guy outside on the landing. 'He still knows,' he had said. He would watch until she slept each time. She had never before felt as safe as during these moments when he was watching over her. But then in the mornings sometimes she could not awaken him. He lay there on those mornings like a hibernating whale. He told her once that he had had a strange fit many years before and had been known since then to sleep for three days on end on occasion. He never knew how long he had slept when his eyes eventually opened again.

'. . . but she did not like it when I left a pool of water on the bathroom floor,' her foreign visitor was saying and she noticed that he had undone two buttons of his

13

orange corduroy waistcoat to reveal a golden emblem on a piece of black ribbon, a circle within a triangle. 'She was German and her friend was too – they had loud voices. She said that even animals clean up after themselves. This is not always true. I am sure that you are in accord with me.'

Lee no longer understood how this person had come into her life. She sat on the floor in the middle of the red carpet and looked up at a picture of an elephant on the wall. The elephant had come from Bangkok and was made up of six lion-men painted on to black cloth in gold and silver and bronze and imperceptibly inter-twined to create the animal. Only the silver tail was a cheat, added on. The rest of the elephant was made up of parts of the human body. The tail had always worried her. This man is not what he seems, she was thinking. He has been sent. What message, what undertow, what trailing shades does he bring with him?

'I have to go to bed now,' she said. 'I'm afraid that I have cheated you. I don't want to let the room at all. It is not you. I am above all changeable at this time of my life. I am so sorry. I can't even offer you a brioche really. Please excuse me. I feel so tired suddenly. Disturbed even. I was thinking of poltergeists today. I think that that must be it.'

'The disturbance in man comes from within and not from without, *chérie*.'

Is this what he was sent to say, she wondered.

'You have judge me,' he continued, 'not – I do not know the word . . .'

'Suitable.'

'Not suitable. You are a lonely woman. I bring nothing bad for you with me but – I understand. I shall go. You must not worry, more will come. You are a woman – *mystique*. I accept.'

He stood up from the deckchair and picked up his

14

gloves and left in one movement like a disturbed shark. It was as if the gods had had to find something with great urgency to distract her and had found only a warped offspring, the fruit of an underworld mating.

The telephone rang.

This house is becoming a freak show, Lee thought as she lifted the receiver. A nice, conventional lodger, a breath of spring air, a . . .

'Oh, hello, darling Conrad,' she said when she heard who it was. 'How is your show?'

She listened for several minutes to the behind-the-scenes torments of the town's theatre's new production, and felt relieved to be drawn into this twilight world of insufficient co-actors and splendid lighting and so-so audiences and faulty backcloths and autocratic directors and general euphoria.

'My dear, how ghastly,' she said at one point. 'Oh, I know, but he's that kind of an actor, all take,' she said at another. 'You must be true to yourself,' at another. 'You must give me some of your delicious spaghetti with basil some time very soon,' she ended. 'Goodbye, my darling.'

She knew when she had hung up that she had sounded brittle and caught Conrad's theatrical tones, and she disliked herself for it. But she had been unsure of herself since Gabriel. She felt like a small island that had been invaded by a major power. She was baffled by the large, metal machines that came down from the sky and frightened the birds away. She knew how she had been but not what she was supposed to become. Somehow her invader had separated her from her island while promising to develop it. She was helpless and floating where before she had been part of her own soil. When she visited the toilet she was jittery, shocked by her sudden separateness and didn't know what to think and had to pray. When she cooked, where before

15

she had had to push Gabriel away to give her space, now to pick up a carrot alone was an almost impossible experience as if she had been in space and had yet to get used to gravity.

'God grant me the serenity . . .' she said to Hosanna as she gathered him up for bed. 'But it doesn't happen. By the time that I'm so unserene that I have to say the prayer, I'm so unserene that it is impossible for it to work.'

She slept in the other bedroom that night, the one with a rug from Corfu that reminded her of Greek peasants. A high, square window looked out on to the yard and when she found she could not sleep she climbed on to the bed and stared up through the small window at the moon.

'How far away are you?' she asked it. 'Clearer than a ghost yet no nearer. How far? We do not know. Not really. Man holds his hands a distance apart and calls that a yard, and millions of times that distance he calls how far we are from the moon. But he does not really know. He just needs to know.'

She scooped Hosanna out from under the bed and took him in with her. His face glowed like an angel's in the moonlight. They lay there together for a long time. Occasionally he licked her nose.

Lord, she prayed, send me a nice lodger and cease these inflows of Gabriel. Send me an angel to cleanse things. Send me a pure being and through its medium let me be exorcized from this terrible obsession. Lord, God, Deus, allow me a little help. Help to free me from these tentacles and to flow again. Bless Gabriel but let me be free. God bless Gabriel and I shall be free. Where are you, Lord? Help me.

She seemed to hear a cry from somewhere in the far, far distance. It was a cry of astonishment, fluted; of mystery, unreal; of pain, violent. The tension flew from her scalp as she listened to it. Something seemed to break, to open.

'God,' she said quietly.

Then she slept.

The dream

She sat and ate seaweed while the sailor-doll rollicked and roared with laughter on the other side of the cave. His mouth was mammoth and red like Salvador Dali's Hollywood-lips couch. He rolled on a round bottom and she wondered whether there were lots of other sailor-dolls inside him, diminishing in size until they became infinitesimal. She thought that if she opened him up to find out he would be angry. His laughter sounded angry even though his mouth was grinning. There was water up to her waist and as she devoured her livid green seaweed she felt that it was being ingested back into the swirling ocean. The seaweed she was eating hung down from the walls of the cave and grew again as fast as she plucked it away.

When she started sinking she thought at first that the seawater was simply stirring the sand beneath her but, after a while, as she sank down and down she came to realize that what was beneath her was quicksand and she could no longer reach the wall-weed. The laughter of the sailor-doll became a gurgle as the water started to lap around her ears and the last thing she heard was a gargantuan cry coloured by despair. 'I love you. I love you. I love you,' the sailor-doll bellowed, as the water rose in one demanding wave over her head. Then there was darkness and her breathing was blocked and her eyes throbbed. Finally everything stopped.

She awoke to find herself in a maze of mirrors, distorting mirrors, some tall and narrow, turning her image into a rippling, underwater scarecrow; some shorter and wide so that she saw in them a fat woman, legs dropsied, midriff like a wobbly barrel; some triangular and made up of triangles so that she was split into pieces, scattered, shattered. In between these mirrors there were sheets of silver and, as she wended her way among them, occasionally a large pane of clear glass. Suddenly at the end of a corridor she saw her mother, dark-haired, laughing, welcoming. Anxious at being alone she ran towards her lovingly, eager. But she had misjudged her terrain and hit a pane of glass through which her mother beckoned joyfully. Her forehead bled where she had cracked it against the glass and she raised her hands and clawed desperately but the window was impenetrable like iron and her mother was still laughing as if her infant had tried to walk and toppled harmlessly. She slid down the glass as her mother leaned forward on to a balustrade and watched her struggle with interest, with warmth, with amusement. When she had reached the floor and lay, bemused and bleeding, she looked to her left into a mirror about a yard from her eyes and saw a strange creature like a sea monster moving around in the water, bulging and hollowing, spiking and denting, raising itself and sinking, in shades of pale purple and grey and silver and black. There was a red mark on the monster's head as if it had been shot and blood was dripping from it downwards into nowhere. She screamed once and then, mercifully, there was nothing.

She heard Big Ben striking and lay in the darkness waiting for it to finish. One, two, three, four, she counted. Five, six, seven, eight, nine. The first one I heard must have been the first. The first strike woke me up. Ten, eleven – I ache. I must open my eyes.

Twelve, thirteen, fourteen. New time-telling. Twenty-four strikes. No, no, no, twelve, twelve only, something wrong. Big Ben's gone wrong – nineteen, twenty, it seems so near, so near to my ear, perhaps it's a radio. Twenty-three, twenty-four, twenty-five. I must find the strength to lift my eyelids. Something wrong here. It's going on and on, perhaps I'm dreaming. One way to find out, must be thirty by now, eyes pressed down by matter, heavy matter. Lift, please lift, damn you, lift. Oh, God, the light, too light and still that bloody Big Ben belling. Up, sit up. Up. Up. Sit up, up, up. Too light. I'm too heavy. Bell too loud. Sink again. No. I'm not. I'm strong. Up. Up. Up. That noise. Up. Ah.

She was lying on the floor of a large, empty room, large as a barn and everything was odd. The room was lit from the ground by bulbous white lamps set in plaster and the walls were made of wooden slats and linoleum. The ceiling was covered by a carpet like the one in her home and as she stood up she realized that she had been lying on a door. She remembered a film sequence with Fred Astaire tap dancing up and down the walls and across the ceiling and thought, so this is how it was done, how clever. A picture of Hosanna lay at her feet but the cat was in a cage and sat eating lettuce like a rabbit. A giant bottle of rum stood in one corner with a grinning red mouth on its label and she couldn't understand why it didn't shatter with the noise. She saw a tall mirror to her right and for some reason felt afraid. To her left there was a window but she could see nothing through it.

She walked towards the window.

Oh, father, she said as she looked out.

She was standing on a level with the top of Big Ben but instead of the clock-face she saw the giant bell itself swinging in the air steadily, deafening her. On the ledge that circumvented the bell stood her father conducting the bell's motion with flourishes of his daily newspaper. He wore his usual trench mac and she could see the dent in the middle of his forehead where a rock had fallen on to him while he had been climbing a mountain-face. Oh, father, she said. I thought you were dead. Looking round suddenly, he saw her and waved so that it looked as if he might topple but all that happened was that his newspaper fell from his waving hand out of sight below them. Mind-manna from the air, she thought, and then covered her ears with her hands for he had started to conduct more vigorously. The sound reverberated more and more as the intervals between the strokes got shorter and she could hear Hosanna screeching. Oh, father, she begged, not this. She felt she would go mad as the noise began to rule her being and her father smiled at her remorselessly and sweetly across the gap that divided them and continued to wield power with his ferocious human tentacle.

No, daddy, no, daddy, no, she screamed but it was only a child's voice and echoed back into the distorted room ignored. Hosanna stepped out of the painting and wound himself around her legs and crawled up her body until his face was close to hers. She could not feel his warmth for the dreadful destructiveness that filled her. As she started to black out Hosanna leapt at the window and was thrown back into the centre of the room and hurtled himself from wall to wall. She looked across at her father once more where he still waved triumphantly beneath the violent sun, then she released her head from her hands, called out to her beloved once more and, accepting this wrath from the gods, let herself go and fell.

Then at last she was with Gabriel. He carried her in his arms down the aisle of a cathedral lit only by rays from the sun which filtered through screens of silk and dispersed themselves over seats of gold. Jazz played and as it played the ancient figures that emboldened the windows moved to its rhythms. Lazarus raised himself and Martha supplicated and Jesus' head fell forward in exhaustion on the cross. All around them sat her people, the people she had loved, but some of them were there as the children they had been and some as the old people they were to become and some had died and smiled at her with mischief. We made it, they said to her, we made it. She shook with joyful laughter in her sailor's arms and throwing her head back saw the face of God which was a laughing face. Gabriel carried her towards a cinema screen at the foot of the aisle and on the screen she saw crowds of film goddesses and giants gathered together in a white, marbled hall watching her, watching him carrying her, watching the entire congregation with pleasure.

'We are celebrated beings,' she cried as they approached the screen and the people started clapping all around her.

'You should never have left me,' Gabriel thundered as he lowered her to the floor and too late she saw that she was the sacrifice. She lay an inch away from a mammoth, celluloid version of Harlow's sweep of white-blonde hair which draped itself over a dinner-jacketed shoulder. Suddenly she was herself again, detached, and when she looked up at the mouths on the screen she saw that the teeth were rotten and knew that foul words were coming from them. When Gabriel had laid her down on the blood-red brocade of the rostrum she looked round at her people, the people she had loved, and watched in rigid isolation as they stood and cheered and lifted their children who were jumping up and down trying to see. She gazed through the illusion to the blood-lust of the wrestling match, the death-wish of the arena, and she prayed to her laughing God who had been betrayed.

The knife tore into her flesh before she was answered.

The exorcism

I

The omelette mixture looked dead, inedible, ridiculous to Lee. It's not cooked yet, she told herself. Amongst the soft, opaque, dim-yellow fluid there wriggled worm-like shapes of clear, unabsorbed slime. She cracked the last egg, one-handed, on the rim of the pretty, primrose bowl with the vine leaves painted on it, let the ochre centre and its more resilient aura slither into the middle of the mixture, threw the shattered shell into the pedal-bin and then beat the eggs furiously until she could see no separation at all.

Her next-door neighbour, Philippa, was sitting on the draining-board kicking her legs up and down. Philippa was perfect, physically perfect. Her body was slight and flawlessly formed, her hair was a soft, golden cap, her skin was translucent, her features delicate and regular and her eyes were light green and shone like a summer field in the midday sun. Even her fingernails were perfect like the ones to be bought in shops, but natural, unvarnished, each curving its way up from a pale, expressive finger to a delicate point. She waved her hands around now as she talked.

'You can't love Gabriel,' she was saying, 'because you can't affect him. He's totalitarian.'

Lee was rubbing her sore right arm with her left hand. It ached after her work with the eggs in the most extraordinary fashion. How on earth do men chop wood all day, she thought.

24

'I did affect him,' she said.

'Pride.'

'Philippa, don't kick the cupboard like that. The backs of your heels will make marks. You don't think they will because you can't see it. But they will.'

The television was on although it was morning and Lee was half-watching through the kitchen hatch. A bright, positive girl was interviewing a vacuous-looking man on whose show a member of the public had recently been killed by a stuntsman's cage falling on him. The press had made a meal of it, the show had been scrapped and the minor celebrity had been left unemployed, presumably at fault, and still entertainingly glowing.

'A chance in a million,' he was saying and Lee could not help but agree with him. She was always surprised that things didn't fall on her from the sky more often, considering how much was up there these days.

Hosanna was mad today, running up and down curtains like a kitten.

'It must be the full moon,' Lee grumbled, melting butter in a saucepan, and then remembered that the moon had been but a sliver the previous night. Images from her dreams charged into her consciousness suddenly and curtained her away from reality. She slopped some of the egg mixture over the side of the bowl and clenched her jaw impatiently. Her tolerance gave out and she uttered a moan and stamped her foot.

'Separation anxiety,' diagnosed Philippa.

'Oh, do shut up, Phil. If you want onions in your eggs then you'll have to chop them yourself.'

'Onions.'

'They're diuretic.'

'Lee, what is happening to you? Marks on the paintwork and diuretics for breakfast. What's happened to your *joie de vivre*?'

25

'It took a flying leap into the quagmire during my last screw with Gabriel.'

'That ri – . . . ri – . . .'

' – ply.'

' – poste is not worthy of you, if I may say so.'

'Well, you may not. You don't know anything. All of Gabriel's people think that they know everything. But you don't know anything really.'

'I'm not Gabriel's people.'

'All right. But honestly.'

'He's not right for you.'

'Philippa, when have you ever, *ever*, known anyone fall in love with someone who was "right" for them?'

'If you love somebody so much that it hurts then you are loving too much. That's a quote, I think. From a book about women and loving.'

'Maybe if you love someone so little that it doesn't hurt then it's not love. You're preaching individuality, intactness, but people let go of these things when they love. Don't ask me to do a liberated woman. I'm not like that.'

'You can love and stay intact. You're too soft.'

'What you can't accept is that *I* accept that *I don't know anything*. People only think they know things. My mother was; she is no longer. And yet she is. Oh, Phil, come and eat.'

They went into the living-room and Lee turned off the television and they ate scrambled eggs in silence, Lee sitting on her resentment and Philippa thinking how impossible it was to talk to someone who had a blind spot, a crazy gap, a fatal flaw. Eventually she put down her plate.

'When I was a child,' she said, 'I used to think that you could look into anybody's eyes, anybody's, and see through them right into their soul. It's quite a common delusion. Then, later, I believed that I had been born to die for someone. To save them, you see. I fell in love with a deaf and dumb man and I planned to spend my life earning and loving and teaching and praying, all on his behalf. I thought that that was what I was here for, that he was something special, chosen by God. Leonard, his name was. He could say both our names, from his throat sort of thing, on a good day. Don't laugh, Lee. But then he started screwing around and I learned that deaf and dumb people are a bad-tempered lot – well, wouldn't you be? – because they get so frustrated and I grew out of that one too. Next I began to worship actors like gods and I'd go and see the same performance again and again, transported, until I learned that the actor, the one I had in mind, was exceptionally polygamous and stingy as a goat and so I let that one go. After that came my Marx and Schweitzer phase but I started getting greedy and wanting them all rolled into one and then somebody told me that we've got to learn to love ourselves, so I tried that but it seemed a bit selfish. I went around being nice to children for a while, being a sort of modern Pied Piper, but I learnt that they're a manipulative lot and crazy for money, literally crazy for it, so I gave them the elbow. But, you see, with all this, and, indeed, before all this, the two happiest relationships of my life were with a schoolfriend called Melanie Smith with whom I used to listen to records of *Carousel* and *Oklahoma*! on an old, wind-up gramophone, and with the hockey-ball when I became goalie of the first eleven. Odd, isn't it? Listening to "When I marry Mr Snow" and wearing white goalie pads. It's the little things in life really. The simple things. Isn't it?'

'I can't imagine you as a goalie.'

'Ah, that's because of the way I look. This is where you are so naive. There's a great, big, hockey-playing

soul inside this fragile frame and there's a lost, searching little boy inside that looming mountain that your
man calls a body.'

'He's not my man.'

'Ah, but don't you wish he was again? Don't you
wish that you could possess him again just like you
own Hosanna? Don't you wish you could eat him just
like you ate your eggs? Don't you wish you were joined
by the umbilical cord again and nobody had the power
to cut it? Neither of you thinks about anything really
except the other. It's like the Hunchback of Notre-Dame
and that gypsy woman, or Beauty and the Beast.
Revolting.'

'He's not as ugly as that. He was beautiful to me.'
Lee spoke simply, positively, but was aware that she
wanted to hit Philippa.

'Exactly, exactly.' Philippa triumphed. She's crowing
like a fairy whose spell has worked, thought Lee. Such
power.

'I shall leave now,' Philippa continued, suddenly
standing, beautiful as a lily. 'I shall go back to my
weaving. The pattern may be complicated but it's a
darned sight easier than you.'

Lee had felt the emotional voltage in the room
heighten to a point when she thought that Philippa
would slam the door behind her, hard, but the door
closed as gently as if there were a baby asleep in the
house.

Philippa, the fortified, she thought, Philippa the
friend, Philippa the priest. How people do carry on.
She sees with a well mind. She perceives with awake
senses. Do I want to awaken? For me my reality *is* my
lack of reality. Living with the dead is my life. I have to
journey through. There is no genie to snap its fingers
and whiplash me out of this world I am living in. I have
to carry on journeying in, in and through and back.

Oh, Gabriel. How beyond them all we were like Lear and Cordelia and the rest, like Queen Christina and her cardinal, Gary Cooper and his Grace, Antony and his Egypt, Salvador and his Gala. All of them and more we were. How terrible to adore like this so that you want to lie in the same grave and share nothing with the world but live above it like Zeus and Hera. And, yes, I know, to become gods you have to lose God and I have been touched by evil. Not touched: it loomed up from the ocean and embraced me in its tentacles.

She sank deep down again, unable to stay alert, and saw without wanting to a giant Catherine-wheel in the sky. Sparks flew from it and shadowy figures cried: 'Look out.' A black dog leapt up at it and growled. She stood in a large yard with a glass of white wine in her hand and it spilt down the front of her red dress when she jumped at the banging noise of a firework.

'Steady on there,' her companion said and as she looked round to smile at him in the fragmented night-sun that was the wheel she saw Gabriel working at the barbecue.

'I've lost my helper,' he cried. The Catherine-wheel was beginning to fail.

'You're making a nice job of massacring those burgers,' her companion yelled at her man. She felt compassionate like a mother and wanted to help him but the wheel had slowed down until its glow had died and she stood paralysed as if frozen in the aftermath of the death of the sun.

'One day the sun will burn up the earth it is now nourishing,' she thought. At that moment a child's bone snapped. She heard the break before she actually saw the child who had fallen at the winning end of a tug-of-war rope. The child's arm had been trodden on, hard, and he now lay on the ground screaming, holding his wrist. It seemed a very long time to Lee before the shadowy adults who surrounded the game moved in on the victim and she wondered why she found herself so static, impotent, so lost. All around her and the scene of the accident sparklers spat white fragments, golden rockets shot up into the blackness, emerald and crimson and yellow pellets soared, squat little gun- powder plants grew amber and silver light-lozenges and purple flames phutted in the gloom. A local MP stood in the centre of the yard, right in the centre, with his wife and three children. They were smiling, willing, charming, but they looked like a family from a breakfast cereal commercial who had somehow found themselves in the middle of a real occasion.

'He's the big "I am,"' her companion whispered, of the handsome politician. She looked desperately around for Gabriel. To save her.

But Gabriel had gone.

Lee no longer wanted to be part of this charade. The mortals seemed miserable and the children cruel and now there was nothing left of the spectacle. There was only the smell of singed paper and sour wine and burned meat and the emptiness is the reality, she thought. The rest is a cover-up. She knew suddenly that she could not live without him. He was her only light; the rest was all sham. People were impostors and children were nothing but the promise of broken bones.

She found him again later that night and took him into her bed. She loved him totally, unconditionally, instantly. She gave him all of herself. I'm taking nothing back except all of you, she told him. So that he laughed. I love you, he said, I really do.

The morning after that first night they bathed together, laughing at their own bodies and the world. Later they went shopping in the markets and bought her red plastic plates and incense and spaghetti and him a copper kettle and a book so heavy that he could hardly carry it he said. On animals, with brilliant illustrations. I believe in Mother Nature he had said.

Then they went to bed again and drank and loved two nights away and then they had a party and then they made a giant salad of mushrooms and tomatoes and sweetcorn and ham and avocado and lettuce and hibernated for a week. Then they had another party. He didn't work for four months. The gods smiled on them and she let go of the past. She felt reborn. She had found her island of happiness and would never swim away from it.

The doorbell rang. Perhaps, she thought, I'm Penelope moping away my life in the underworld, hearing bells occasionally but never rescued, never redeemed, destined to live lightless, buried, alone. When she opened the door she stared.

'You look just like Philippa,' she said. 'Who are you? Are you her brother?'

'No, I'm nobody's brother,' her gentleman caller said. 'I saw an advertisement about a room.'

'Oh, yes. Come in. I'm so sorry. It's a compliment, by the way: Philippa is my next-door neighbour and startlingly beautiful. It really is very odd – why, you could be twins. Except for your hands. Your hands are workmanlike. How very odd.'

'I mess around with motor-bikes actually.'

She was going to offer him an armchair to sit in but he had already decided to settle at the pinewood table. He leaned his chin on his right hand and looked up at her.

Lee was charmed. The resemblance between him and Philippa was remarkable. They could double up and play Viola and Sebastian, she thought. It's not just features, it's a similar – radiance. They vibrate at the same level. Yet he occupies his own space while Philippa wavers all around hers and he dances where she stumbles and sings where she lectures and lives, just lives, where she prods, activates, teaches. He's like a fairy skylarking in attendance, Lee decided, where Philippa is like a clumsy, banished elf struggling for attention. He's the diametrical opposite of Gabriel, she realized. David and Goliath, a silver fish and a killer whale, a yacht and a battle-ship, a piece of silken crochet and a sleeping-bag, a flute and a drum.

The young man was asking her about the room, about his chances of getting it, she suddenly heard.

'Oh, I don't see why you shouldn't have the room,' she said in answer to him. The doorbell rang again.

'Can I get it for you?' he said, seeing that she had settled into a chair.

'Oh, yes,' she replied.

It was Philippa, and Lee was delighted. As they stood on either side of the door looking at one another she felt as if a magic elixir was being created, ready to cure a disease.

'What a beautiful young man,' Philippa was thinking.

'What a beautiful young woman,' the young man thought, and, unaware of their own narcissism, they sat on either side of the pinewood table for all the world as if they really were twins, recently separated and reuniting in astonishment.

'I'm Philippa,' Philippa offered.

'Oh,' he replied, 'I'm Larry.'

Lee got up and picked up a piece of cross-stitch tapestry from the top of an old record-player and sat down in the rocking-chair, her back to the two young people. She gently rocked the chair to and fro as she started to work on the head of a unicorn in white embroidery cotton.

'What star sign are you?' Philippa was asking. She's been reduced by this encounter, Lee was thinking. She's become 'young'. She flounders.

32

'I'm not telling,' Larry teased.

'Lee's Aquarius,' Philippa went on. 'It's why she's both wonderful and loopy. Well, it's true, Lee, just go on with your sewing.'

'Are you Taurus?' asked Larry.

'Oh, no, you guessed. Lee, he's a miracle, and you are never to scoff at the stars again. How on earth did you know? Nobody's ever guessed before.'

'I'm a Taurean too,' Larry said.

There was a silence after this during which both of them tried to integrate this information but could not. It is eluding them, Lee thought, like the swinging end of a bell-rope that has to be grasped before it will ring the bell that will awaken them.

'I don't scoff at matters of the spirit,' she said as she threaded her needle with gold to start embroidering the unicorn's eye. 'I only detest charlatans, cheap make-believe, truth-evasion, lies.'

'Oh, la-de-da,' said Philippa, 'see how harsh she is.'

'She's right,' said Larry.

'Well, she always thinks she is,' said Philippa rudely. 'Do you believe in reincarnation?'

'I don't see any reason why you shouldn't live here, Larry,' said Lee, biting off a piece of thread.

But Larry was absorbed in Philippa.

'I met a woman once,' Phil was saying, 'at a weekend houseparty in Devon. It was in an old house with a minstrel gallery and everybody seemed to be running up and down corridors in and out of one another's bedrooms. One evening at dinner, just as things were going quite tamely, a toad came into the dining-room. A real toad. We were eating off silver plates and suddenly there was this toad. It just bounced in from the garden. I was going to pick it up and put it outside again when a woman, a psychiatrist's wife, stopped me. "No, no," she said, "don't touch it – you will burn

33

it. Brrring me some ice." She had some kind of a mid-European accent. Anyway, everybody rushed out into the kitchen and cook found some ice and wrapped it up in white cloth and then this woman picked up the toad and put it back in the garden but with the ice in her hands. She said that their body temperature is such and such a million times lower than ours is and that we burn them, literally burn them, if we touch them. Isn't that brilliant? But here's the best bit. I'd rather taken against this woman – she was frightfully solid and know-it-all and not funny, you know – and to be difficult I asked her how she knew this, thinking that she would quote out of some boring manual or other. But no, she didn't. Do you know what she did? She lifted her chilly hands into the air and proclaimed: "I rrremember what it was like to be a toad." Well. It turned out that she and her husband were experts on reincarnation and ran a sort of reincarnation centre in Switzerland and she had been an Egyptian princess – before, you know – and written books about it. She was quite credible, actually, quite legit. She could describe things like the difference between horses now and then, stuff that is virtually inaccessible. So. You see. You never know. I think Lee needs a bit of reincarnating, don't you, Larry? Sorry, Lee. I won't carry on. But honestly. Loopy. Wonderful, but loopy.'

'Anyone can concoct stories about horses,' Lee said with unexpected fierceness. 'Spiritual matters are . . . beyond us, intangible. Not fairy-tales. Hidden realities.'

'Oh, la-de-da,' Philippa laughed.

'Philippa, do stop saying "la-de-da" like some deep Southern belle. I don't know whether you heard me before, Larry, but I see no reason at all why you should not live here. Do you like this?'

Lee had risen and moved to where he sat at the table and was showing him the completed unicorn's head.

'I like unicorns,' she said, 'don't you? Such singular creatures, I always feel.'

'Lee, nobody who hasn't known you for at least a hundred years is going to appreciate oblique and esoteric . . .'

'Hush, Phil, and let him look.'

But Larry declined to look at the tapestry and turned his head up towards her instead. The irises of his eyes were almost large enough to exclude the whites and they were coloured light green like grapes and flecked with gold. Suddenly she switched on a yellow lamp that stood by her on the table and moved the snake-like stem so that Larry's face was spotlighted as if on stage. He flinched but withstood the glare and held Lee's steady gaze. Philippa was laughing in the perimeter of shadow that surrounded the light and Lee felt oddly stable looking down at Larry as if she were surveying an actor from the height and comfort of the gallery.

'Oh, no,' she said eventually. 'There is no reason on God's earth why you should not live in this house.' It isn't me doing this, she was thinking. What is happening? She switched off the light and laughed as if she were innocent, fun-loving. She felt controlled, at odds with everything, fearful. Larry blinked as the light left his face and laughed to show his complicity. Philippa clapped her hands. Nobody spoke for a while. The silence was bearable like a musical pause. Larry took Lee's tapestry out of her hands and looked at her newly embroidered unicorn.

'Thank you,' he said eventually. 'It's a strange world, isn't it? Unicorns don't exist, do they? Not really.'

He looked up at her again. She had never seen anything as unspoiled as his face before.

'I like it though,' he said. 'It's pure, elegant, supreme. It's OK.'

Lee smiled at him.

'I'll be very good,' he said to her. 'Thank you.'

And then he smiled at her as if for the first time, a smile that made her think that he had been touched by God. She gazed gently back at him.

'Thank you,' he said again. 'I knew I'd come to the right place.'

II

Sometimes Gabriel's ghost was so physical, so vivid, that Lee would almost cry out to Larry to warn him as he moved through it between the kitchen and the living-room or walked over it as Gabriel lay on the carpet in front of the television. Hosanna could see it too, and would prick up his ears as he sat on her lap and focus on Gabriel moving around by the sink or fixing the green curtains at the window. He would gaze for a long time and, when Gabriel had finished his tasks, would settle again until the ghost reinforced itself somewhere else a few days later.

But Larry saw nothing except the tap dripping in the bathroom and the rug missing from the doorway and the absence of a cat-flap and his own image, his own image everywhere. His narcissism touched Lee. The world was his lake and echoed him constantly. He was as sensitive about his body as a proud owner of its pet's and was perpetually asking her to look inside his ear to see whether there was something amiss – she saw nothing but pink perfection – and wondering about the freshness of his lungs in the atmosphere – she assumed that they were like his ears – and surveying the immaculateness, the flatness of his belly in her long wall mirror with its carved, wooden frame. And all the time Gabriel lived with them, reverberating, massive, and she and Hosanna hid their secret and said nothing.

The four of them lived together and Lee kept her counsel and Hosanna stayed in contact with the spirits and Larry larked around and looked longingly at himself in convenient reflecting surfaces.

One day she herself was looking in the mirror, and her sailor came up behind her and put his arms around her waist, and stared hungrily at her joyous face. Then he took his arms away and roared with laughter and drew comic glasses round her eyes on the glass. Someone was speaking, she realized, someone who was neither Gabriel nor her.

'You never listen to me,' Larry was complaining.

'I'm sorry,' Lee said, turning, back with the living. But when she looked at the mirror again the stain of spectacles was still there and she had to wipe it off with a cloth so that Larry would not see.

'What are you doing?' he asked.

'Cleaning the mirror,' she replied, truthfully enough but with deceitful happiness in her heart. Let go of him, they said to her, let go. But he would not let her, her stubborn sailor, he held on to her as the walls held on to the moving air within her house.

'I want to have a dinner party,' Larry said. 'Will there be a problem?'

'Why, no,' Lee said, folding up the cloth. 'Let's combine. It's so long since I had people to dinner. Why don't you have two and I'll have two and then we'll be six?'

They decided on the following Friday for the party and Lee said that she would make a chicken and pasta and fruit and nut salad and make borscht and buy black bread and invite Philippa and Conrad if Larry would buy cheese and wine and serviettes and invite two friends of his own.

'Do you think they'll mix?' worried Larry, and she thought he meant the food but he meant the people.

'The more the merrier,' she smiled back, hugging the seventh guest to her. 'We've got twins for a starter.'

'But theatricals and arty types, and my lot?' he pondered.

And nautical visitors, she savoured, and quickly switched her thoughts to cheap chicken and walnuts from the market and whether the Rising Dough shop sold black bread for the borscht or only brown wholemeal.

On the day of the party her lodger was busy tending to the needs of a Mrs Brown whom he felt he had nothing to offer but was obliged to visit anyway. 'Try being a social worker,' he would moan, as he modelled his new, pale-blue running trousers. So Lee did all the shopping herself, wearing her fur coat and her black Russian-looking hat. The stall keeper cheekily hummed 'From Russia with Love' as he filled her bag with bananas and apples and onions. 'Swipe him one,' a fellow marketeer suggested, but she smiled enigmatically, remembering Gabriel. 'Skinhead,' the kids would yell at him as his hair stood on end in a gale. 'I was a skinhead before you were born,' he would bellow, and only she knew how it hurt him. He understood the weather, did Gabriel, as only a sailor could, and from the angle and force and temperature of the wind and the shape of the clouds would predict the nature and time of the storm. But he couldn't control it, for all his knowledge, and it would lift his hair into bristles so that he looked like Desperate Dan and she couldn't help but laugh until his fragile ego wobbled and then he shouted and then she loved him more, more than when he was intact.

All day she worked. She pinned old movie stills to the black beams so that the guests could play at guessing what they were from and gazed for too long at a film-still of Peter Finch and a male lover, pondering the

39

nature of sexual passion. She put silver candles on the table and orange and white blossom in the corners of the room. She laid out a selection of records from Harry Roy through theatrical speechifying to the Beatles and Scott Joplin. Then she cooked pasta and shredded chicken and chopped fruit and nuts and sliced black bread and made beetroot soup and prepared sour cream and a cheese board and polished wine glasses and put butter in lemon-coloured dishes and made salad dressings and laid the table and set a serviette decorated with a Groucho Marx face by the side of each place. Then she decided that there might not be enough food so she went out to buy potatoes to put in the oven to bake an hour before the guests were due. She was lonely. 'Such a middle-class way of carrying on,' she thought, and remembered how Gabriel and she had revelled in roast beef and two veg, and concocted casseroles of liver and sausages and baked beans. Always together. Working-class fodder. And lots of laughs. Together.

When she had done all she could she went to the bathroom and wept for a while and found herself raging against her lodger for being young and clean and free of spirit and unsure because he had never faced death. She felt suddenly dirtied by death, ashamed of the knowledge she had gained when she witnessed the cessation of breathing that marked the end of her parents' lives, sad and sullied by the separations she had lived through. 'Party, party,' she yelled out to break the spell and Hosanna ran from where he had been sitting watching her. She lost him then and had to search and found him eventually curled up amid the wiring in the back of the record-player where he hadn't hidden for a long time, not since two dark-haired people who were into black magic had come to dinner and he had disappeared for half a day until she found his secret hole. She sat and rocked him for a while until he felt all right again and then went upstairs and dressed herself in a low-backed, jade green jumpsuit and gold pumps and gold hoop ear-rings, and felt exotic. She wore a dark make-up base and painted kohl on her inner eyelids and a golden circle on her forehead to make her look Indian with her brown hair, and dabbed an oil-based perfume called Roma behind her ears.

Then she sat cross legged on the floor of her bedroom and meditated. Until Larry burst in.

'What are you doing? I've got to change. Do you think brown velvet trousers is going too far? Confucius or Conrad or whatever you call him was on the door-step. He called me "darling". I'm not sure about the brown velvet trousers now. "Darling!" I like the candles but the kitchen looks a bit messy. Come on, Lee, you're the hostess. Do you think he'll call John "darling"? I'm a bit worried: John's having trouble with his girlfriend at the moment, and he might go the other way. No, not the brown velvet. I'm going to wear jeans and a white shirt. And a medallion. God, no, not a medallion. Jeans and a white shirt. Lee – '. She stood up, a bit trance-like. 'You look – beautiful. This is all a bit much for me. First I'm called "darling" by an actor and then there's this apparition of loveliness. I'm going to wear the brown velvet trousers and the medallion. What's the red stuff in the fridge that looks like blood? Sorry, it's the beetroot soup, isn't it? Come on, Lee, it should be red-hot by now – I'm going to change.'

'Darling,' Conrad cooed as Lee entered the living-room. 'Just look at this stomach – hasn't it got minute? Here's some Blue Nun – the coffers are empty, heart – for a Blue Angel.'

'Your stomach's enormous, Conrad, you drink far too much beer and do you really think you should call young social workers "darling"? You must try to remember that some people are normal. Ish. I adore you. Do be kind. I'm going through adolescent love-trauma and I cry when they play "Smoke gets in your eyes".'

'Where's Hosanna? Where's my pussy? Come to Daddy, Hosanna. How I have missed you and how cruel your mistress is. My one and only love, keep purring in my arms. You know you can't love people, Lee, because they are frightened of life and I think they are quite right and should beware of everything, especially camp comedy, the Communists, erotic fiction and you. Poor, bleeding heart, but I'm here now, love me, why don't you love me? But you don't, you see, you neglect me, and chase after the butch, the macho, and the brutal. Silly Lee, you look wonderful, you are a gem – why do you tarnish yourself by mixing with trash?'

'Oh, Conrad, there is no "trash". Here, I've opened the wine, have this glass and do settle. Do I really look all right? I wanted to look Indian. I've always thought that India might be my true spiritual home.'

'Ah, vino. Lovely, darling. When, oh when, are you going to stop searching? The answer lies within, cuddles, the answer lies within.'

'Don't call me cuddles, Conrad, you picked it up from that stringy comedian who behaves like a long-distance runner. Do settle. Philippa's coming and she's all right, but there are two straights as well and I don't want you to frighten them.'

'Frighten *them*? But I'm terrified, darling. Shaking. A nervous wreck. We're all horrified by one another, we humans, and there's an end to it, but I shall be a good boy and sit quietly stroking Hosanna who is, when all's said and done, my only true friend.'

Conrad was looking good, Lee thought, despite his

paunch. His face was round, soft and glowing like a baby's and his gentle, grey eyes were laughing despite his verbal cynicism. He always looked to her like an infant who had grown bigger and bigger and then stopped growing without changing much. She loved him, and was both sorry and glad that he was gay, and hoped that he would not get drunk.

'He just stops giving,' he was saying of a fellow actor, 'in the middle of a scene – what can you do? And I've noticed that he doesn't do it when there's anyone important in, isn't it shameful, no sense of responsibility to the audience, no sense – your doorbell's ringing, darling.'

It was Philippa, who had brought flowers because she didn't drink as it was bad for the soul, anemones in one hand and carnations in the other. Lee took them from her and kissed her and whispered in her ear: 'Be nice to Conrad,' because she knew Philippa considered him decadent and damned.

'Good evening, Conrad,' Philippa said as she came into the room and bestowed a kiss on his bald patch, saint blessing sinner, and then called out to Larry whom she had seen going in as she walked up the hill with her offerings.

'Come out, wherever you are – I know you're there, *doppelgängers* don't disappear, and I want you to see my new dress.'

She was wearing something lime-green and minuscule, with silver sandals adorning bare legs that looked like the stems of a slender plant. Lee felt jealous, lumpy, and tried to let go of the feeling as she arranged the flowers in the kitchen. Philippa had let in Larry's two guests, she saw, and they were hovering, looking transparent and shy, and she too called up to Larry who leapt down the stairs. All in white, she noticed, which lifted her spirits and made her smile. One of his

43

friends who was called John, she heard during the introductions, was as beautiful as Larry, but dark as a panther, cool as a wooded river. She glanced at Conrad whose head was near the hatch where she was working and, sure enough, he had transferred his attention from her cat to the young man who had melted into the rocking-chair; his expression was quieter, more thoughtful. She flicked a pink anemone at him through the hatch and it hit his cheek so that he turned round and winked at her. As she carried the flowers into the other room she saw that the other boy had an arm that was twisted, very twisted, like a clever but grotesque sculpture, and his face was oddly formed like a plasticene model interrupted by a child's clumsy fingers. Her heart went out to him, and she showed him her anemone arrangement and asked him if he liked it. His answer shocked her.

'Anemones are a bastard flower,' he said in an irritable voice. 'They have neither the innocence of the daisy nor the legitimacy of the rose.'

Lee hurriedly asked Conrad to pour some wine, and prayed for the evening.

Suddenly she saw Gabriel. He sat naked, at her desk, reading something he had written at the typewriter. He was angry with the person he was writing to. But when he looked round at her he smiled as at a companion-general in a war. She became desperate with lust, standing by her guests with her anemones in her hand, trying not to look down for her sailor's erection. She walked to the desk and put down the vase and by the time she had done this Gabriel was gone.

She looked round swiftly to check whether the others had seen him but Conrad was pouring wine and chattering, Philippa was settling herself into the crimson beanbag, Larry was moving around in the kitchen,

John was sipping his drink and testing out her rocking-chair and the lad with the twisted arm was hovering, uncomfortably. She felt thankful that they were taking no notice of her. Her sudden head movement would have seemed unnecessary, paranoid.

'Do sit down at the table,' she said to the rude young man. 'We shall have to picnic it, as you can see. What is your name? I've missed the introductions.'

'My name is Demian,' he replied, sitting opposite Conrad where she had gestured, 'and yes, I do mind about my arm. Just in case you were wondering. I actually do mind.'

'Don't be a bore, Dem,' Larry called through the hatch. 'Lee, I'm dishing out the borscht.'

'Fine,' Lee said, 'fine.' And to Demian, 'You really mustn't mind about your arm here, you know.' But he winced at that, and she thought, this has nothing to do with ego, and continued, 'I'm thinking that really the big difference is that it must make it more difficult to handle things. Tiring.' She wondered whether Philippa had really outgrown her passion for partially disabled men but she seemed oblivious of all this and sat like a springtime sprig in a bed of roses, contemplating her coincidental twin. Then Lee dared: 'Byron had a limp, you know.'

Conrad, who had downed his glass of wine in one, objected. 'There is nothing romantic about limps, dear girl. I played a character in Birmingham with a limp and a stutter and they said I was overdoing it. I'd been number one golden boy until then.'

'Acting – the art of compensation and over-statement,' said Demian.

'Oh, really – ' said Philippa.

'If you paint a cathedral, it doesn't mean that you are compensating for not seeing it,' said John.

'Not quite the same thing,' said Larry.

'There are more things in heaven and earth,' said Lee.

'Cheeky young pup,' said Conrad, pouring more wine.

'To elaborate is to deny what's real.'

'What about Lowry?'

'This is philistinism.'

'The conversation's above me – here's some borscht, Phil.'

'To some, inner truth is realer than reality.'

'Have you seen Maggie Smith in the latest Cocteau?'

'Modern telecommunications have made art superfluous.'

'On the contrary, the need for redemption is more evident than ever.'

'Don't be pseud, Phil. The sour cream's not sour enough, Lee.'

'It's your bitterness, Demian, not your arm,' John said morosely.

'Blow winds and crack your cheeks!' bellowed Conrad on his third glass of wine.

Lee was laughing, thinking of Gabriel's log. He had built it out of practically nothing for the local amateur dramatic society and it had sat resplendently on the stage like something fetched straight from the nearest wood, so real, yet with touches of the bizarre, so brown, so greyish, so admired, so solid. The leading actor had believed in it so heartily that he had kicked it in mid-speech and got his foot embedded in it. Gabriel the workman, Gabriel the megalomaniac, Gabriel the king in his kingdom, Gabriel the reliable. Until the crunch. Until the crunch. I must stop this, she thought, Conrad's getting drunk: I must be careful for him. He has taken against Demian. Wobbly limbs cut no ice with him. What a metaphor. I'm tight. On one glass of wine.

'Are you a social worker like Larry, Demian?' she asked.

'I'm a servant,' he replied. 'I work with the terminally ill.'

The silence that followed this remark was not an embarrassed one. It's as if he has heroically outlined himself, Lee thought, become the most significant member of the group. We think that he can teach us something. But Conrad was on the attack like a crazed bird beating a cuckoo out of its nest.

'Pretentiousness is the cocaine of the caring classes,' he soliloquized. 'We are all terminally ill, dear boy, don't you know? We are all dying. Always have been. Until you see that, you will not live. It's life that kills. Life is killing us moment by moment, and until you are humble enough to accept that you will never be truly aware. You will go through our comic, existential garden with your shears and you will never water the lupins. I'm drunk, darling Lee, I'm dying. Only your love will save me. Wrap it around me like a Cupid-woven shawl and then let's dance together in this maze we call living, searching for the centre which we all know is death. At least Byron went to Greece and made a name for himself. I'm sorry, dear boy, I don't mean to be rude. But if you erect this wall around yourself we shall be forced to throw stones. And Lee is in love. With a man. With a great lump of meat known as man. I wish I was a man. Lee languishes for love and I gaily die out my life. Food, lovely Lee, food. I have been playing a cad for too long and have forgotten my table manners.'

'Shush, Conrad,' Lee said disapprovingly, and cleared away the soup dishes. 'We are going to have some nice chicken salad.'

'She condescends. She condescends. But a cat may

look at a queen. A tramp may criticize a prince. A knave . . .'

'I don't think anything is terminal,' said Philippa. 'I think that we are all part of one eternal cosmic soul.'

'You have not suffered,' stated Demian, as if it were a scientific fact. 'You know nothing.'

Larry had gone beetroot-red like the soup, Lee saw, as he sat next to Philippa on the carpet, but Philippa herself was as alert as a newborn bird and was tickling his ankle with a silver-sandalled foot, excited by the nonsense, unafraid of the conflict. The wine seemed to have depressed John. His chin was on his chest. The rocking-chair was still. He brooded. Lee wondered about him as she served the salad. He was like a De Niro, a Pacino, one of the dark ones, one of the damaged ones, one of the paranoid celluloid heroes. I'm interested in someone other than my seaman, she thought. But no, it's only because he reminds me a bit of him, that gloomy bit, that deep bit, that bit that dominated when his head sank into his shoulders and his mouth turned down and the light went from his eyes, that bit that took over when he resisted and turned inwards and moped. How you would have hated this, Gabriel, how you would have hungered for the sea and the sky, the hurly-burly and the heave-ho, the teamwork and the solitude, the unpredictability, the freedom, the danger of the waves. Such an elegant and delicate little salad with its walnuts and its lemon dressing and its fresh lettuce base and its morsels of white fowl-flesh. I want to eat red meat with you. Hunks of red meat torn from the bone. I want to lie with you on deck and screw beneath the stars. I want to pull in the anchor with you and save the whale with you and bear a big child with you and live with you and know that we will never die. I want to cut you and lick the wound. I want to trawl with you and devour the sea-flesh. I want to fuck with you and never stop. I want to gorge on life with you, I want to take your strength from you and give you my care. I want to breed with you like monkeys and fly with you like the birds. I want to sail through with you like the fish. I want to love you. I want to love you again, Gabriel. I want to love you.

'Chicken up,' she said, passing plates through the hatch. 'Do be a good boy, Conrad.'

But Conrad was weeping, opening another bottle of wine and letting tears drop steadily on to its yellowed glass. Then, within seconds, it was over and he was sauntering around the room pouring the almost clear liquid into the guests' glasses like an insouciant Greek waiter. She marvelled at her friend and abhorred the expression of disgust she saw on Demian's face.

'Eat up,' she said, 'There were going to be potatoes but I got lost chanting mantras. Eat, drink and be merry, for tomorrow we intervene in social crises, we perform for the masses, we weave at the loom, we grieve for lost lovers and we bring salvation to the suffering patient. Don't be a cry-baby, Conrad. I adore you, but Demian just can't stand false sentiment. Or art,' she dared.

She put on some music while they ate and the conversation moved from the complexities of the dys-functioning family to fertility rites to developing acting styles to the persistence of Aids to Harry Roy to the nature of joy to the repressiveness of English Fascism to the astrological outlook, and, finally to Lee, herself, to her tendency to withdraw from the group, but, ultimately, to her graciousness as their hostess and the deliciousness of her food.

'Thank you,' she said, 'And now we will play the film, play, book and song game because you're drunk and ripe for laughs and nobody shall deny me.'

Philippa went first, kicking off her sandals as she rose from her beanbag. She indicated that it was a musical film and then stretched her perfect fingertips above her eyes horizontally as if scanning the horizon.

'Search . . . look . . . yonder . . . land ahoy.'

She dropped her hand and looked enquiringly around flapping her arms in the air.

'Oh, where, oh, where, oh, where, can my true love be?'

'Play properly, Conrad. This is the first word.' Philippa started looking under the table and lifted the edge of the carpet, rather desperately.

'Hiding place . . . treasure . . . lost horizon . . . where . . . where, oh, where, oh, where, can my true . . . shut up, Conrad . . . where there's life there's hope . . . where? . . . somewhere . . . somewhere? . . . it's somewhere . . . it's somewhere . . . the first word's somewhere . . . somewhere . . . over there . . . it's a rainbow . . . "Somewhere over the Rainbow"? Oh, well done, John . . . well done, Phil, so you . . . why were you . . . shut *up*, Conrad.'

John's was *Wuthering Heights* and he cheated by doing 'withering'. Larry did *French without Tears* and Conrad made a great show of *Kismet*. When Demian stood up, Lee felt nervous.

'A film,' they shouted as he rolled the camera. For the second word he looked gormless and drew a circle over his head.

'Saint,' Lee guessed.

'Monk,' from John.

'Holiness . . . Pope . . . goodness . . . goodness? . . . smaller . . . good, the second word's good. Oh, good . . . fourth word . . . he's pointing his thumb some-where . . . he's pointing at Conrad . . . off? . . . failure . . . sorry, Conrad . . . he's looking disgusted . . . sour . . . off . . . bad . . . yes? . . . bad . . . good, good, bad

. . . seven words . . . seventh word . . . oh, my God, he's pointing at his arm . . . this is torture . . . whose idea was this? Hurts? . . . the good and bad and . . . ugly . . . ugly? Honestly, Demian, *The Good, the Bad and the Ugly* . . . hooray. Well done. Lee, come on, you must do one . . . oh, yes, you must . . . entertain us, my pretty.'

She did *The Old Man and the Sea* with ease, acting old, acting a big man and swimming the breast-stroke in the air, and they got it almost immediately and then she flopped on to Conrad's knee and he laid his wine-filled head on her breast and somebody wiped a smear of black kohl from her cheek and she felt like a child again and thought of how Gabriel had nursed his little girl to sleep when she had been tired and fading away. The game had brought them all together, and even Demian's morbidity had become accepted. They drank coffee happily, Conrad and Larry had a brandy, Philippa flirted with John to tease Larry before leaving, then they ordered their taxis and suddenly they were all, even Conrad, devastatingly, magically, irreversibly, gone.

Hosanna had retired to the bathroom and was sitting on the windowsill, squat like a buddha, gazing out into the night.

'Do you disapprove of us, my angel?' she asked, exalted by wine and overbearing, and took him down to the kitchen to give him some of the leftover chicken. She took bits of chicken to bed with her and fell asleep while still chewing.

That night she dreamt that they were all, Larry and Philippa and John and Conrad and Demian and herself, dancing the hornpipe on the deck of a warship that was ploughing through a storm, but Demian's leg was tragically maimed and would not keep in step and Conrad was shouting at him like a great actor-manager,

51

and the tears were streaming down Demian's face, or so she thought, until she realized that it was she who was crying, crying for the sick one, praying that her tears would heal his wound. Then she held Demian in her arms and they danced together until they dissolved into one another in the storm. Philippa was dancing alone like Tinkerbell while Larry and John monkeyed up the mast and Conrad, suddenly bearded and old, fought the winds and the rain with his clenched fists.

And then Gabriel was there. Ten times larger than any of them, he descended on to the deck of the warring vessel like the giant from the top of the bean-stalk, like Captain Bligh, like Neptune, like her love. He found her where she clung to a rope that was curled up in a corner of the iron ship and picked her up and carried her through a secret tunnel down through the floor of the ship, down through the underwater crea-tures, deep into the earth beneath the swirling sea.

Then, and only then, did she feel safe.

III

'Lee, do you know a big, red-bearded man? Looks a bit Renaissance?'

Lee had just come back from shopping. It was the second weekend after the dinner party. She had detoured through the town's central square on the way home and had sat down on a bench, raising her head to the trees. The starlings were disturbed, swirling around in S-shapes and parabolas and unexpected clusters. When they finally settled in the branches of a tree there were hordes of them, so many that they looked like fruit overburdening their source, ripe to be plucked.

A teenaged boy had approached her, holding out his hand, mutely begging. 'Have I asked you before?' he asked when she refused him money. She answered no, without thinking. 'Rotten, fucking cow,' was his reply. The depression, she realized, had given beggars the right to alms, first time round, but at the second attempt you were free to withhold your support.

The man sitting at the other end of the bench took a quarter-bottle of whisky from the pocket of his torn donkey-jacket, twisted off the gold tin top and took a swig. He put the opened bottle down next to him and smelled the top. She worried for the safety of the bottle, knowing it was his food. A debilitating feeling of fatigue overcame her. She felt like a mother whose sons kept dying in overseas wars. The starlings are free, she thought, why aren't we? The man's hair was long and stringy and his eyes blazed like a charismatic actor's. 'Why?' he said, but it was to himself or another power, not to her. A few drops of rain fell. She looked again at the bottle, standing like a soldier on the wooden bench. She smiled, thinking of whisky and water. The man screwed the top back on to the bottle and stood up. 'Why?' he said once more, and walked away towards a bus-shelter. She shivered and thought of Hosanna. The man kept his hand in the pocket where his bottle nestled. I shall cook a pork and prune casserole tonight, she decided, and feed Hosanna with fresh liver.

The rain had stopped. An old woman with a hunched-up back and a walking-stick was beckoning to her with one hand a few yards away. Lee jumped up and went to her. The woman had dropped an orange pen on the concrete and was unable to pick it up. 'Thank you so much,' she said as Lee handed it to her. 'I can't complain,' thought Lee. When she got back to the bench she saw that she had knocked over one of the shopping bags when she had stood up and a carton of eggs had dropped to the ground. Two had broken and egg-yolk oozed into the cracks of paving-stones. Twelve pence, she reckoned; perhaps if I had given ten pence to the beggar this would not have happened. I would not have started up so guiltily and . . . the Lord works in mysterious ways.

'Lee,' someone said.

'Oh, hello,' Lee replied, pleased. It was a generous and bubbling woman called Meg who lived in a caravan and whom Lee had met through the Labour Party and liked enormously. When Gabriel and she had been a couple they had run into her one day when there had been a freak storm. They had all laughed together. Lee had felt like a sailing-boat between two galleons.

'What are you doing around these parts?' she asked.

'Well, I'm avoiding Broad Street because of the cranes,' Meg replied, and Lee saw that there were tears in her eyes.

'Cranes?' she smiled.

'Yes. I'm terrified of cranes. I know it sounds nutty but I've always been frightened of cranes. I used not to go out at all if there were any around. I don't understand it. I thought I'd got over it but it seems to have come back. I have to skirt round Broad Street because they're demolishing and there's a great big red one and a yellow one and I'm just terrified. I know it sounds nutty.'

'Not at all, Meg, you're the sanest person I know, except for living in a caravan on the edge of a cliff. Perhaps you were brought by a crane and not a stork?'

Meg beamed at her gratefully, and passed on, promising phone calls, safe from the cranes.

I like cranes, Lee thought, I like their power, I like the way they scoop. I like their angularity. I like their useful monstrousness. It's people I'm afraid of. I don't understand them. I learn and I learn and I learn, but each one of them is a faraway mystery and I tremble in my ignorance. Except for Gabriel. Except for Gabriel. Except for Gabriel. Gabriel's not a mystery. Gabriel I know.

When she arrived home she had found Larry polishing his shoes at the table. His question about the bearded man alarmed her. Something had gone wrong. Her ghost had materialized. She sensed sacrilege. She put down her two shopping bags and picked up the shoe-polish.

'Why, it's Cherry Blossom,' she said, 'you sweet, old-fashioned thing. You will be eating grape-nuts at breakfast next. A big man?'

'Yes.'

55

'Why?'

'Why what?'

'Why do you ask me if I know a big man?'

'You've got to relax yourself, Lee, because you're too . . .'

'Nagging produces a counter-force.'

'I'm not nagging. I'm asking.'

'Yes, but why?'

'Because I want to know.'

'Why do you want to know?'

'Blast these shoes. Why don't they have shoeshine boys any more?'

'Busking and shoeshining aren't allowed, except in a boom.'

'Do you know him?'

'I think I know who you mean. This is a funny neighbourhood, you know. Lots of characters. Odd forces.'

'It's just that he was passing the house as I came in and he looked at me really strangely. And then he looked up at the front window. Sort of searching looking.'

'Well, that's all right. As long as he didn't throw stones.'

'So you do know him.'

'I didn't say I didn't.' She took the shopping into the kitchen. 'He's a roofer, if it's the person I'm thinking of – he was probably inspecting the roof. The folks are like that hereabouts. Property-conscious. Property first, politics next. I shouldn't think he was searching for anything elusive. Low imagination count. What's happened with this fridge? It looks like an igloo.'

But something had changed. Something had crawled from under a stone. A smear had appeared on a painting. Fog had slipped through a crack into the ivory tower. A tumour had manifested itself. Fine fabric had been scarred. An alien object was threatening the organism. I knew, Lee thought, as she stacked tins and packets in the food cupboard, I knew. That's why I waited in the square. That's why I delayed coming home. I will not let this happen. I cannot let this happen. The spirits must be kept safe within the house, otherwise they will rot and eventually die. Larry's the threat. It's Larry who's doing this. He's toxic. Sugar-coated. Toxic.

'I'm going to defrost the fridge, Larry,' she said.

But he had gone out of the front door, banging it, leaving his shoes on the table which she'd always believed was bad luck. Hosanna had been sleeping, his pink nose hidden by a paw, on a chair by the table. The bang of the door woke him and he reached himself up on to the table and started sniffing the newly polished leather.

'Bad shoes, Hosanna,' she said. 'Bad, bad shoes.'

Behind fresh eggs and bacon and milk at the front of the fridge she found a pile of dates covered in green mould, and a piece of Stilton turning grey, and an older lump of lettuce wrapped in newspaper. Water had dripped on to the paper so that it had become sodden and merged with the lettuce leaves. The result looked like an insidious, grey-green growth lopped off an otherwise healthy young tree to protect its trunk. She gagged and cleared it all away.

'Sick day. Sick, sick day,' she moaned as she wiped the shelves of the fridge and turned down the temperature knob so that the intrusive crusts of ice would melt. Hosanna started to smell the debris where she had put it on the marble top of the kitchen dresser and she shouted at him so that he darted out into the yard. She threw the mess after him and then thought, I'm cracking up, and retrieved it and buried it deep in the refuse bin. Then she went out and picked him up and cuddled him and fed him on the cream of a new bottle of milk.

'The Gabriel out there is the skeleton and the chilled flesh,' she thought, 'The energy's in here.'

She turned on the television to watch the midday news and learned that an impasse had been reached between the American and Icelandic leaders during their discussions about the reduction of nuclear weapons.

'Black day, black day,' she mourned, and switched off and played Mozart. She felt cold, although the central heating had been on all morning, and took a large brown woollen shawl out of a drawer and wrapped it round her as she sat in the beanbag and listened. The music soothed her for a while but the needle stuck in a groove suddenly and she wept in response, despairing. She took the record off.

'I can't tap the energy,' she thought, 'and everything, but everything, is out of joint.' She clenched her teeth to hold in a scream. 'Larry, what have you done? You saw a shadow, that's all. You saw the shadow of the mountain and you let it into the cave and the fire has gone out. What have you done, Larry?' She shivered. 'What, oh what, have you done?'

IV

The steam hit her like a white-hot slap. Perspiration sprang through the skin of her body instantaneously. She was surprised and sat herself down more carefully than was necessary on the stone seating. Her shoulders dropped as the tensions began to ease and she raised her face to the condensed water on the ceiling, trying to relinquish control. The steam was so thick that she could not see through it and she thought she was alone in the room.

'Men,' she said, her voice sounding hollow.

'Don't mention men to me,' she heard. 'I have lived with my husband for twenty years and still I do not know him.'

The accent sounded mid-European and as Lee became more accustomed to the steam she made out the face of the owner of the voice. It was a middle-aged face, deeply wrinkled around the mouth and on the forehead, and artificially tanned. The eyes were bright blue and heavily mascaraed in navy and the woman wore a pink ribbon in loosely permed hair that was coloured almost to a shade of orange. Her brown stomach showed stretch-marks but her body was in good condition, small-boned but compact and muscular. She sat leaning against the white-painted wall in a corner diagonally opposite Lee. Lee laughed.

'That's wonderful,' she said.

'It is true, my darling,' the woman replied. 'I have to be careful what I say – I come from Poland and we are very outspoken in my country and I have noticed that in this country you people take offence very easily. But I have to speak my truth. Twenty years I have lived with the same man and still I do not know him. We have never slept apart and still I do not know him. I have borne his child and still I do not know him. I am Catholic and cannot divorce but I do not want to divorce because I do not know him well enough to want to divorce him. You think me strange but it is not I who is strange – it is the truth that you find strange. In this country you cover the cake with poisoned icing. I speak truth because I cannot bear to live otherwise.'

Perspiration was running down Lee's body and she knew that she needed to shower but didn't want to leave.

'No,' she said carefully, marvelling at how the steam conducted the sound. 'No, I don't think you are strange. I, myself, am considered a little eccentric. I'm not sure what this normality, this centre, is that people speak of. No, I don't think you are strange. But I wonder. It seemed to me that the man I recently left was the only person that I did know.'

Drops of condensed water fell on to her head from the ceiling and she thought, I must leave soon or I shall melt into the atmosphere. The sweat was dripping from her face on to her breasts which were already glistening with water like orb-shaped fruit in the rain.

'Then you are deluded, my darling, because you do *not* know him. Women open themselves up to men but the men, they stay like rock, whatever they say, so that this,' she threw one hand up into the steam, 'and women's tears do not touch them.'

'My man was soft,' Lee asserted.

'Ha! So why did you leave him?'

'I don't know. I sensed danger.'

'Because you did not know him. There, there was the danger.'

'We knew each other's very souls.'

'And where is he now?'

'We were a different breed.'

'The men are one breed, the women another.'

'I think I needed to feel my own pain again.'

'Ah. The solitude, this is pain.'

'He took away all my pain. It was a kind of tyranny. Kind tyranny.'

'You are very brave, my darling. For twenty years I have known the same man and yet still I do not know him. Without him – I would be – terrified.'

'I must shower.'

When Lee pressed against the door it would not open so that she panicked, standing in the enveloping steam. I'm trapped, she thought, I can't get out. I shall stifle. But the door gave and she stepped into the shower-room where the air was clear again.

She stepped under a running ice-cold shower.

'You've got a nerve,' someone said, as she took the shock.

'I lost my virginity twenty years ago,' a squat, blonde woman under a hot shower was shrieking. 'In a tent. I remember the blood on the grass when I came out afterwards. I didn't feel a thing. Well – I liked it but, you know.'

She wouldn't talk like that in the bus, thought Lee; there's something about all these naked bodies. She looked round and saw this woman also had stretch marks on her stomach. She left the shower-room and went to sit in a comfortable, brown chair in the rest-room. She closed her eyes and meditated.

She saw Gabriel pinning holly to one of the black beams in her house. He was nearly as tall as the ceiling

61

and hardly had to reach. 'If you pin it so that it hangs down, people will catch their hair in it,' she was saying. But he knew his own mind, did Gabriel, and persevered so that the holly adorned the bottom edge of the beam like a curving curtain pelmet. 'I think I'll come off the pill,' she said when he had finished. He bellowed with laughter after she had said it, but later was serious and said, 'I wouldn't like to have to see the suffering.'

'It's hard work as much as anything,' she replied. 'I want us to create something together. There'll be another little Gabriel in the world.'

'There'll be another little Lee,' he reproached. But she could only see little Gabriels, wearing small red anoraks and sporting hair that stood on end no matter how she tried to brush it down. Little Gabriels, out of control most of the time and impossible to educate, but with a fund of kindness that led them to rescue and foster wounded animals and plague her with them in the home. Later that Christmas Gabriel had drunk a bottle of rum watching a pirate film on the television, and she had known then that, really, it was all over.

'Hallo.'

Lee left Gabriel with his pirates, opened her eyes and focused on a sign on the wall in front of her, which read: 'WILL CLIENTS PLEASE SPEAK MORE QUIETLY IN FRONT OF THE BEAUTY ROOMS.'

Her new companion was speaking rather loudly, Lee thought.

'Did you see that Alan Ayckbourn play on television last night? Very good. It can happen, you know.'

Lee had switched on the television the previous evening and had watched the Ayckbourn for a while. Two rather hysterical women had been talking in a suburban living-room, the one brunette and hawk-nosed, desperate for approval of a new pair of shoes, the other auburn and bright-eyed, and equally desperate about an undeclared affair her absent husband was having. The thought-processes of the women interlocked brilliantly with no meaningful communication of any kind. She had been unable to bear the women's pain and had switched off quite quickly, despite the cleverness of the actresses.

The woman sitting next to her looked pregnant but wasn't, Lee decided. She had the sort of belly that has produced perhaps three or four children and never managed to forget its importance or let go of its previous function or recover from its distension. Two rolls of flesh formed an outsized necklace that hung beneath the navel. The facts of the flesh are inescapable, thought Lee, and not always entirely commendable. Yet when she changed focus from the stomach, which was the first part of this new individual to catch her attention, to the face, which was the second, she immediately fixated on what she saw there. The nose was rather hooked, slightly splayed, a 'tribal' nose, thought Lee, the skin brown like wrapping-paper but pearlized as if touched by moonshine. The hair was black, cropped short, the mouth looked like a casket holding mighty documents, and the eyes – the eyes were blue like electric shock-waves and held Lee as the eyes of an O'Toole or Cooper hold the audience when in close-up, like magnets, obliterating backdrops, Chinese plains, crazy broads, plots, accompanying scores, Orson Welles, everything. Lee turned her head away, looked down at her own navel and tried not to think about her mother. From this face came the question about the Ayckbourn play.

'No, I didn't,' Lee answered, and waited.

'I've got a cousin like that one that Mary McAnally played. Ooooh, she is a bitch. Alan Ayckbourn would have a heyday with her. She's the sort of person who'd

63

criticize the flowers you brought to her funeral. She was terrible to Tom, she really was. Terrible to him. Poor Tom. It can happen, you know, what they got up to in that play; it can happen. What a shame you didn't see it. You'd have enjoyed it. All over a pair of shoes, I ask you. A pair of shoes. And yet it can happen. Oooh, I do think he is a good playwright, I really do. When our Sandra left Wally he went just like that. He did. You wouldn't believe it but he did. The thing is, Alan Ayckbourn can make you laugh about it, can't he? I mean, that bit in the broom cupboard – oh, you didn't see it, did you? Well . . .'

Lee awoke lying on the top of a green, green mountain, being looked down upon by the largest face in the whole world. The face was female, sculpted, golden, mellow, ideal and framed by a lion's mane of light. Lee lifted herself a little towards her goddess and rested herself on one elbow, looking up like a child, expectant. The perfect lips parted. Lee knew that here it was, her key, her salvation, her message of infinite wisdom and enduring joy. 'Speak,' she smiled. The goddess spoke. 'Clean your shoes, one shoe in the bedroom means ten years in the penitentiary, our Gladys was the maddest it can happen if you let it, clean your shoes, your shoes, mud sticks, six and tuppence, please, oh no you're not getting away with that you're not getting away with that, it can happen. Fred's having it off with Diane and it can never get stuck on again, that's what happens if you – it can happen, the dreadful already has, you mark my words, I think they're very nice, dear, now don't you worry, that broom will never sweep again, don't let him get away with it, it can happen with your shoes off, I should take him back, dear, he who hesitates is lost, you can get lots of laughs with the vicar, should have seen it, one good turn deserves another,

64

niggers in the broom cupboard, Mavis was just the same, what a shame . . .'

'Miss Pembroke, Miss Pembroke . . .' Lee jumped and opened her eyes to find herself alone in the rest-room apart from one of the girls who worked there, who was leaning over her and gently shaking her shoulder. The girl wore mauve false eyelashes and a pink tracksuit.

'You were talking in your sleep,' she said. 'I thought I'd wake you.'

'Oh, I'm so sorry,' said Lee. 'What on earth was I saying?'

'Nothing too terrible, it's all right, it was quite sweet. Something about mystery or misery and "Gabriel, Gabriel, Gabriel," you kept saying. "Gabriel" and people and knowing something. Nothing really. You must have been dreaming.'

'So silly. I'm glad no one was here. Thank you. I'd better go and do some work.'

'You're welcome.'

Lee suddenly felt so sad that she thought she would never move again. The sadness seemed to extinguish her as if she had no real eyes or fingers or genitals or teeth or frown-lines or kidneys but these were just slight irregularities in the sponge that was her sadness. This is too much for me, she thought, I am drowning. It won't even come out of my eyes, because my eyes themselves are the sadness. This sadness is like the sea and is claiming me; I am gone. I have no power. I must fight the sea with hatred. Feel my violence, feel my spite, kick my own spine and spit at the others like that loony lady who walks around town looking smart and knocking people's hats off. Hatred.

Ten minutes later in the gymnasium downstairs Lee reflected that if she threw one of the dumb-bells she was using at the wall-sized mirror and it shattered into a hundred pieces around a central trauma, she would wake herself up and everybody around her and get into the local papers. Instead she dutifully lifted each weight in turn from the shoulder high into the air, staring steadfastly into her own cow-brown eyes. She saw a tall woman in the mirror, shapely, body closely covered by a black leotard scooped deeply at the neck. The hair fell to just above the nipples that protruded slightly through the black nylon, and a silver streak on the right side of her head matched the silver of the dumb-bells when they caught the light. She saw one entity, one woman, the reality of her – rather forbidding, she thought. But there were two of her inside, and it awed her. Inside Lee could see a wraith, a transparent, whitish wraith, shivering, willowing, wafting. And around this wraith there gathered forces of darkness, Lee thought, as if a strongly penised Satan, black-bodied, black-blooded, black-souled, had disseminated himself into threatening clouds. Lee watched the wraith, trembling, trying to flee, melting in the midst of this power. It's Gabriel, she thought, Gabriel's inside me, he's power, I'm in his power, God help me, I thought it was love. Oh, love me, Gabriel, please love me, don't overpower me, love me.

'Since I married my husband I've only met two men, that's in seven years, that I've even been tempted with,' said the voice above her. She was lying flat out on her pink bath towel along the lower level of the dry-heat sauna. There was a notice outside the sauna asking people to keep quiet in consideration of the other clients but the two women who were discussing men were ignoring it. Lee wanted to slap them. 'They're me, me, me-ing', she thought spitefully, 'and no man would even look at them.' Despite the two gossiping women she felt more relaxed. She liked the sizzling sound of the water as it hit the stones when someone threw it from the bucket. She liked the hard feel of the wood

66

under her back. There was a smell of lemon like bath-salts and she could hear the slap, slap, slap of flesh against flesh as somebody tried to stimulate her circulation. She liked the way the perspiration slowly emerged through her skin looking like deposited dew and she liked to be aware of the naked bodies lying in so many different postures around her. 'It's an anatomical artist's dream,' she thought. An African girl one level up was lying on her left side, her right leg bent, with green and brown towels over her hips and head. Lee wondered what the towels were for. Her body looked like dark mahogany, and the lights and shades created by the dim bulbs were silver and sludge-green. Lee found herself gazing at the pubes of a woman a little way along from her and thinking about undergrowths and mazes and secrets and magic and dirt. 'Oh, Gabriel.' She turned herself over on to her stomach.

'My husband doesn't think like that,' the unattractive woman was saying.

'God grant me charity,' Lee prayed. 'Oh, Gabriel, I could only love everyone when I loved you. You drew me through the undergrowth out into the light and then left me bare and hurting. Now I hate. Oh, Gabriel.'

Then she emptied her mind as the sweat poured.

The sun was shining when she walked out of the health club. Down the hill to her left she could see the ocean which was mid-way between calm and turbulent. The whites of the tops of the waves were lengthy, pretty, insistent. 'They look like invisible ink,' she thought, 'which, when lifted, will reveal . . .'. An ugly black dog barked harshly at her from the basement patio of the house next door. 'You can't touch me,' she triumphed, 'I'm intact. For the time being. Cleansed, all toxics out. I'm free.' She turned to her right and set off for home, all thought and feeling evacuated along with her energy and her sweat, in touch only with the irregular paving-stones, the light-rays interrupting the pink-grey clouds, the number-plates of cars, the lines on the faces that passed her, the name of the day, its date.

But she knew that her ghost still awaited her.

V

'So I just said: "Poppycock". This man/woman thing is an illusion of the West. No self-respecting Zen-Buddhist spares a second thought for it. Zen-Buddhism's beyond thought, anyway!' Philippa was cleaning silver nail varnish from her nails with a substance whose odour reminded Lee of some exotic flower turning rancid. The varnish held tiny, solid pieces of silver metal which stayed on the pieces of tissue Philippa was using and scratched the next nail she treated. Consequently she kept digging into the supply of tissues that Lee kept on the marble slab in the kitchen. Philippa was wearing a black kerchief which covered her hair and was tied at the nape of her neck, a knee-length black T-shirt and black straw sandals. From her right ear there dangled a long silver cascade of tiny orbs. She looked as if she could have stepped straight out of an urchin's game on the street of a Northern Italian village or off the front cover of *Vogue*. She had been talking for several minutes about a party she had been to the previous evening.

'But they're top-job people, you see, and they're all in family units so they don't understand, their minds are closed. I was talking to that presenter of that alternative-politics programme – what's his name? – and he said that he'd got annoyed with a colleague because she criticized his pink bow-tie. Why can't they let one another be? I don't think we understand spiritual matters in the West, do you? His girlfriend was chatting up some big-shot drama critic at the time as well. If that's love, give me a few mantras. How did this all happen, Lee? People setting themselves up as the philosophers and artists and intelligentsia and other people setting themselves up as their assessors? Do you think that each lot really wants to be the other lot? I think so. We're never satisfied with what we've got in this society, are we? It's the age of anxiety because everybody's wanting. Well, I don't want anything. I exist. Shit. This nail-varnish. I only did it to impress that lot. Now it's like trying to scrape car paint off. I kept trying to put them in bed all with the wrong ones if you know what I mean. The six-foot, ascetic literary genius with the tubby socialist from *The Newviews*, and the culture-vulture's punk daughter with the Professor of Philosophy, from Jedburgh. He's so intelligent that I don't think he would even take his glasses off before doing it. Aren't I being naughty, Lee? Still, if sex has got to exist we might as well try to do it properly. I don't think that I could do it with anyone whose bones stuck out. It's got to be like cuddling up to a cushion as well as doing that terrible, animal thing. I know somebody, male I might add, who's so randy the whole time that he can't concentrate on anything. Literally. Not anything. He's a crossword compiler as well, so I suppose he must delegate. Some novelist went up to a critic last night and thanked him for a review he wrote on a novel of his in about the year 1900 and congratulated him because he got it right. I love it, don't you, Lee? "I read your review of my article based on your review of my novel derived from Dickens . . ." I'm sure those people aren't being themselves at all really. Intellectuals have a weakness for the prurient, I read somewhere. Of one thing I am sure and that's that all problems, not just some but *all*, start either in the head or in the genitals. Don't you think, Lee? Lee? Oh. Oh, I see. Oh, Lee, Lee, is it me? Lee? I'm serious now. Don't. Lee? What is it? Oh, I'm so sorry. Sorry, Lee.'

Lee had suddenly stopped in the middle of washing up a pottery casserole dish, quietly placed it on the draining-board and sat down on the kitchen floor. She held a damp, grey cloth in her lap and tears were pouring on to it. The tears were moistening her hair so that it clung to her cheeks, and they didn't look like stopping. Hosanna padded down from the steps that led up to the patio door and sat beside her, lifting his right paw and placing it on her thigh. Philippa's hand jerked forward anxiously and knocked over the bottle of varnish remover. Hosanna's ears lifted at the sound. The smell was alien, threatening.

'Blast. Sorry, Lee.'

But Lee hadn't noticed anything. Philippa got up from the chair she had brought into the kitchen, went to take the cloth from Lee's lap, decided against it, and started to wipe up the insidious liquid with tissues. Lee's weeping was silent like water spilling over the edge of a suicide's bath. Philippa felt afraid as if war had been declared, suddenly and inappropriately, over the radio.

'How could you be so silly?' she scolded at the varnish remover. Then she glanced down at Lee as if she thought Lee might take it as a remark against her. She wanted to kneel down next to her friend but felt that she would be trying to get close to the untouchable. Always before, Lee's face had seemed strong to her, square-boned, attractive but guarded, the forehead lined like that of a chess-player, the mouth soft like that of a maternal woman. Now it looked grubby, collapsed and marked like a very old deck of cards. Philippa's fear was exaggerated, as if a bridge had started to collapse under her. She felt like a child at the scene of an accident who knows nothing except that flesh was not made to be torn. She thought about cathedrals, her father, wooden cradles, strong things. She wanted to cry too.

The tears stopped. After a moment or two Hosanna moved back to the step again. Lee's hand went to her forehead. Then she stood up, turned to the sink again and picked up the rust-coloured casserole dish from where she had left it. When she had finished cleaning it she started on an aluminium saucepan. Philippa sat down on her chair again, crossed her legs, adjusted one sandal, and looked at her friend's back for some time.

'I have these dreams,' Lee said, as she worked with a red plastic scourer. 'I'm not sure what's real any more. I miss Gabriel so terribly. In the dreams I am sinking or searching or sacrificing. Always something engulfing me, always something surreal to make out, always my blood at risk. Sculptures and dolls and statues and bells and odd buildings, and sometimes Hosanna's there and it's nearly all right but these things are laughing at me, never with me. Never with me, Philippa, never anything or anyone with me. Seaweed and my parents back from the dead and objects come alive and sort of leer at me and sometimes I joyfully feel as if I'm going to sink to the bottom of the ocean forever, but I wake up and then I don't know what's real. These dreams are realer to me than this house. My father and Gabriel are realer to me than you or – anyone in the now. There's something wrong. With me. Maybe I'm having a breakdown. Gabriel held me together for so long. I miss him so terribly. He's here, I know – '

'What do you mean, "he's here"?'

'Oh, I . . . I'm talking nonsense. I'm all right.'

'No, it's not all right. What do you mean, he's here? Lee, you know he's not here. Oh dear. He's not here,

Lee. Oh, Lee, you're as large as life. You're not having a breakdown. We love you. You're just being silly as my mother used to say. Don't be a silly person, Lee. Have a laugh. You're going through something. Oh.'

'There's something darkened about me, Philippa. Gabriel weighs on me . . .'

'But look at Hosanna in the sun. Look, Lee.'

The glass of the door to the patio was bumpy, mottled and had deflected a ray of sunlight on to Hosanna as he basked on the step, making him golden, religious. Lee turned her head to the right to look down at him. And there was Gabriel, sitting on the stairs that led up to the bedrooms. His chin was in his oversized hands and he was beaming. He had a half-beard and he looked dirty, as if he had just been working with hammers and bricks and wood and chisels. He put his hands on his knees as if to lever himself up.

'Oh, please don't move,' said Lee. 'No, not you – oh, Phil, he is here. Not is. He's gone. But he was here, just now. Looking filthy, you know, the way he did. I've got to sit down.'

Half an hour later Lee had told Philippa everything, curled up in a newly acquired floral armchair in the living-room. Philippa had taken her black kerchief off and twisted it around her fingers as she sat at Lee's feet. She listened purely as if she were receiving information intended to entertain, not to disturb, from the radio.

'. . . so, you see, he *is* here,' Lee finished. They sat quietly for a while. Then Philippa kicked off her sandals and started to pad around the room in bare feet.

'Don't pad, Philippa, or I shall think that you don't believe me.'

'Well, I don't. No, that's not treacherous. I mean, I suppose I do in a way. I believe you – how shall I say? – the way that one believes the most miraculous actor

73

on stage. Because they believe it, you do. But I know it's not true.'

'I'm not acting.'

'Yes, but neither is the actor when he's being brilliant.'

'No, it's different. I understand – the actor talks to a non-existent character, or even a dog, on the stage, and he makes it so real that the audience sees it, you actually see Gabriel. I'm not pulling anything. I'm not existentially deceiving. I'm just saying that he is here. Gabriel is in this house. If sometimes, then always. It's just that I'm the only one who can see him. If I were acting I would be trying to make people see him. But I'm not. I accept the reality. He is here but nobody *can* see him, except me.'

'Well.'

'Do you think I'm mad, Phil?'

Philippa sat quiet for a while.

'No,' she eventually said. 'If you were mad you'd be calling us all mad. You would be arrogant. So no. But you're not right: Gabriel is not here. He's in his workshop. Maybe he's with another woman by now. Sorry. Or he's asleep in his pad, or he's boozing. That's the most likely. But he's not here, I can assure you. His bullying, lovable, bloody self is elsewhere.'

'Oh, Philippa, you're prejudiced.'

'You sit there and tell me that you can see men or ghosts or apparitions that no one else can see; you deny all evidence that the man or ghost or apparition is actually elsewhere and therefore cannot be here; and I am prejudiced? Think, Lee.'

'Well.'

'Well.'

'Philippa – there were marks on the mirror over there once, left by his fingers, the perspiration on them. I had to wipe them off. Truly.'

74

'OK. What was he, your second Gabriel, doing with his mucky old fingers all over your mirror?'

'He was drawing glasses.'

'He was what?'

'Outlining joke spectacles, you know, around my eyes, from behind. It was meant to be funny, you know Gabriel.'

'And he did this when he wasn't here?'

'No, he did this when he *was* here.'

'It's a moot point. Oh. You're laughing. Oh, good, that's something. Oh, Lee, you're laughing.'

'It's the relief of telling someone. I can see the funny side: it is funny. If he's not here it's funny, and if he is here it's funny. But, Phil, you've got to believe me: he is here. I don't know. Perhaps I am cracking up. But once I saw him lumbering down Ward Street, you know, opposite, and he was here as well, messing around with the television. And the television picture changed, Phil, it changed, it changed, it changed.'

'Lee, take it easy. So a television picture changed at the same time as you saw your ex-lover walking down the road opposite. So what?'

'I swear to God that Gabriel was in this room mending the television. Philippa, I don't know. This could be an emotional thing. But, if so, why don't I see him in bed with me? It's not like that. Listen. I read a book – I don't know – some metamorphosist or something who went to live on an island – anyway, he believes, he says that there is something – that things are caught in light and space waves, that we don't die, that it's all still here, but that we just can't see it. That the future's here too, in some sort of space and time-lock, but we just can't catch it visually, experientially. Oh, God, I can see: you think I'm lovesick and am having hallucinations. And I am. Lovesick. I took Gabriel into myself and loved him more than myself and maybe you're

75

right and I just can't let him go, but it's not like that, Philippa, I swear it, it's something else, a force – something wonderful if only I weren't so alone with it, something terrible unless I learn to understand it. He's here, Phil. He comes, which means he's here all the time but I just don't tune in. *I see him*. Material body, organism, behaviour, vibes, expression, self: I pick up on all of it. I swear. Oh, God, let me not be mad. How can I ever stop loving him when he's always here?'

Philippa felt something gripping her in the area just behind her breastbone which sent a message up to the area somewhere above her eyes which were growing tired with concentration. She did not know what the message was: Lee in this state was no longer a lovelorn friend but a trauma. She could not bear it. She felt as if she might be struck by lightning if she stayed where she was. Something too fierce was attacking her from the inside. She was discussing problems in Lee's living-room but she could have been standing in front of a giant black door in the middle of a forest. The door would not open and she had nowhere to go.

'Lee, I have to get a breath of air,' she said.

'Oh, Phil.'

'I'll be back in a minute.'

Lee listened to the patio door closing quietly, and felt ashamed, ignoble, as if she were embarrassed about having had an epileptic fit or as if she had broken wind in the middle of a fairy-tale. She had expected too much of Philippa. She was not sure enough of her own sanity to take these risks. She had exposed her most vulnerable part to a vicious archer. The arrow was flying towards her and she bled in anticipation. She wanted to beg Philippa for understanding, for belief. I'm an older woman, she thought, I must stop this. How I hated my elders for their frailty, for making me feel responsible for them. I must tell Philippa that I was

76

joking. And, of course, that's all it is really, a joke sent by the gods to test me. How they must be laughing on their Olympian level. She closed her eyes and pictured the gods. She felt a sudden, soothing pressure on her knees. When she opened her eyes again Philippa was kneeling in front of her looking up at her. Some of her nails were still silver, Lee noticed, and some were so clear that she could see the blood through them.

'I'm going to get some help, Lee.'

'Oh, no, Philippa.'

'I can't leave you with it and I can't deal with it. I feel as if I'm going crazy.'

The line between Lee's eyebrows was short, deep and intense, Philippa now saw. Like a scar, she thought. Perhaps this is a very sick woman.

'I'm not sick,' Lee said.

'I know you're not but – let me phone Conrad, Lee.'

Conrad stood in front of the figure-length wall mirror in his basement flat and tried to successfully knot a maroon cravat.

At the same time as trying to knot the heavyish material he peered down at his stomach.

'You distend,' he said, 'you're a beer barrel. You disgust me.'

The knot looked crooked in the mirror and he started again, concentrating. To the left of him in the mirror he could see the remains of last night's meal. The dinner conversation had become so hectic, so involving, that when his guests had left he had groped his way into his bedroom and fallen asleep, drained. He could see six glasses, wine-glasses, on the green and white table-cloth. They seemed to be positioned at random as if the guests had been playing a game with them and not sitting around the table in an orderly fashion. One of the glasses had fallen on to its side and a red stain had spread from it on to the tablecloth. The stain looked like a squashed tropical insect. From where he was standing Conrad could see limp, darkened lettuce and mushrooms that looked like sleeping slugs and unfresh tomatoes in a large wooden bowl in the middle of the table. A brie sat on a wooden slab, hardening at the edges. The stem of the rose that he had decorated the table with had bent over so that the pink flower seemed to be praying, bowing, deferring. Begging for forgiveness, thought Conrad. Whoops, that's the wine. Irrational remorse. Lee thinks I have a problem, I can tell. But how else, how else can I make life bearable?

As he finished tying the cravat into an acceptable knot he saw that one of the cheese-knives had stuck to the table linen by virtue of the butter that had been left on it. Maurice, he thought, who claims such pure-mindedness. Wine-stains and grease-stains. This depression. One day the pit will be so deep that no one and nothing, not even God, will be able to scoop me out of it. What was Maurice saying? Something about being corrupted before being born because of the original act. Biblical. Sometimes I think that we don't make things any better with our homosexual antics. Why do I keep thinking about Maurice. He's got inside my head. It's as if he's still here. Am I going mad? Who else was there? Here. Then. Now. God.

He turned from the mirror and started to clear the table. Jo, the lady-hypnotist, he thought, Sandy, the lady publisher, Cara, the lady pianist and the three free spirits. What is the world coming to? He screwed up his face as the hot water from the kitchen tap scalded his hand. Strange how they cling. No, Charley's not a spirit. Neither are Maurice and I really. Just struggling organisms. Lonely. That's the trouble. Charley's not lonely. Of all of us, Charley is the least lonely. I wonder why? The women are lonely because they are professional women and they have no sustenance. Maurice and I are lonely because . . . Because nobody understands us, and we hate ourselves for needing to be understood. Charley isn't lonely because he's like a diamond, solitary and rare, yes, but hard, intact and sure and everlasting. When Charley dies it will be like the end of an object or the closing of a book or the last date of an epoch. It will be a full-stop. There will be none of this decay, this sadness, this tailing-off, this mess, this mingling of feeling. A diamond with an ending, that's Charley. These people crawled into my head last night and now they control me like ghosts. Perhaps Charley'll crack one day, while Maurice and I just carry on malingering. What did Jo say? There's a place deep down inside yourself where you are always safe. Then why do I always feel as if I am falling off the edge of a cliff? I must get these people out of my head. How did they get in there? I had a dinner-party, that's all. Got to get my act together, otherwise they'll crowd me out. Where's the panache gone? Down the rubbish-chute with the salad remains.

Lordy, lordy, loo time. This lock is stiff, must mend it, handy enough, just. Not so much butch as brave. The loo seat's cold. Nothing's perfect, I suppose. Oh, just look at yer up there. He sat and squinted through watering eyes at a coloured, enlarged picture of himself on the wall ahead of him. He was dressed up as a pantomime character in the picture and was posing. He looked rather less plump than he felt now. A well-rounded performer, he thought. Why did that queen, Angus, tread on my laugh on Saturday? It's a beautiful laugh, beautiful. I build to it during the lost-in-the-wood speech and then it starts a bit uncertainly and then they really get it and it hits the show like a trumpet solo. Incompetent queen. No soul. I'll tell him. Ouch.

79

God, you look beautiful up there. Not like down there. He stared down at his knees, then stretched his legs out and gazed at his calves and feet. What a load of rubbish, he thought. Skin white, no moisture, hairs black, no glow, bones big, no beauty. Ugh. Better to be drugged than have to face it. My feet look like discarded lumps of sponge. Horrible hairs on them, even. There seems to be a myth alive in my head and muck dying down there. Ugh. Ghosts are a gift maybe. Life is a film – why shouldn't I watch it? But they seem more alive than me in here. Maybe they are. Maybe I'm the ghost. Maybe they're alive and I am dead. Maybe ghosts steal back and invade you to inhabit you, because they're lonely. Why am I thinking like this? What's that? God, the phone. That'll be them, the real them, with post-mortems. I blacked out a bit last night. I hope I didn't say anything rude to Sandy. She gets my goat some-times with her long, strong nose and her self-assertion. The ghost gets my goat.

A half-empty bottle of red wine stood on the tele-phone table and he picked it up and drank from it with his left hand as he lifted the receiver with his right. He gagged on the sourness so that he could not speak into the telephone. He could hear somebody talking urgently at the other end but his mind was still scram-bled and he could not decipher the words.

'Blast,' he said. 'No, sorry. Is this Sandy? What? Lee? Oh, it's not Lee. It is Lee? Look, who is this? Oh, Philippa. Hi. Sorry. Hung-over. Divine but impossible party last night. Keep growing chrysanthemums, dar-ling and wearing daisies, the hooch is not good for you. What's the matter? I'm not being facetious . . . I haven't heard anything yet, I told you, I'm still recovering. Of course, I'm listening, I'm not hearing, that's all. Actor's licence, dear, superhuman editorial skills. You sound irate or alarmed or something. You weren't here last night and I've forgotten, were you? If you arrived while I was in black-out, I apologize. Drop my mask? Why should I? Oh, it's important. Lee's seeing ghosts? Aren't we all, darling. What's she on? I am serious, darling, I'm so serious I feel like bursting into tears. You don't know what it's like to be a lonely artist, wandering gipsy, bum . . . oh, I know I'm no good, you don't need to tell me . . . look, can you . . . what kind of trouble? Well, but I've just been conversing with ghosts myself. On the loo, you know. Oh. Yes. No, it's all right, I'm with you now. Can I speak to her? All right. No, of course. If it's real trouble. It sounds like something out of a horror movie. I suppose I mustn't laugh? No. No. I mean, I love her, you know that. If it's serious. I've got the show tonight but . . . yes. I'll come over. You're sure she hasn't been making wine out of your dandelions? You don't grow dandelions? I'm a bastard? No, I'm not, Philippa, I'm your favourite breed. Look, if Lee is in some kind of trouble, I don't care what it is, I'm with her. I'm coming over. Tell her big, real Conrad will be with her soon. About half an hour, maybe a bit longer if I walk. Well, she's not going to jump out of the window in the next hour, is she? No, it's all right. I know. I'm not sending it up. I've felt, I've noticed, just recently . . . she's not what she was. Odd. Something different. "There are more things in heaven and earth, Horatio . . ." Philippa, I am not "full of myself", I'm worried about Lee. Hang up now. I'm coming over. Oh, and Philippa . . . I love you too.'

Fifteen minutes later Conrad was walking along the high street towards the hill where Lee had her house. He felt suspended between one drama and another. From O'Neill to Williams, he thought. But no, not with Lee. Lee's real. Really Lee. What can all this be about? Sweet Lee, sailor Gabriel, and the ghost. God alone knows what she saw in that brute. Lee's one of the chosen and he's one of the damned, for my money. No, I'm jealous. Oh, women. I'm the sort that they need and I can't handle it. Lee. If it had been anyone it would have been you, sweet Lee, with your mighty reserves and your kissed and kissing face. Must be still drunk. I hope I'm some good. Want to help. Want to help Lee. What is this all about. Ghosts. No, a ghost. The sailor, did she say? What a strange day. Lee's no Ophelia. She can cope. Yet it's bad, must be, or she would have phoned herself. Pull your belly in, you tart and get useful. Say a prayer for Lee. Sod Sandy, drat the depression, narks to the narcissism, say a prayer for Lee. I'm needed, ye gods, I'm needed. Help me to help her. Help me to help our Lee.

There was a loud report somewhere outside the house and Lee clutched her pillow. Her bedroom was darkened, brown velvet curtains pulled to against the daylight. One desk lamp was switched on at the far end of the room, one candle, round, red, squat, burned on her bedside table. The candle flame threw shadows, like paper-ash, thought Conrad, on to Lee's face which was tired and childlike and rested its cheek on the pale-lemon linen of the pillow-slip. She had been crying again and her mascara had been washed away and she looked like an eleven-year-old waking up in hospital after an operation. She still had her clothes on but was covered by a grey duvet. A shroud, thought Conrad. Blast this depression. Lee's alive. Not well, but alive.

Philippa sat cross-legged beside the bed, as if meditating on the carpet. Hosanna was asleep on top of the duvet. Conrad was settled in an armchair in a far corner and felt like a witch in a coven. No, he thought, like an investigator in the dark, surveying his subject through a one-way mirror. Lee's hand relaxed on the pillow. They had all been sitting quietly for some time, waiting. Waiting for Lee.

Hosanna suddenly woke up, sat up and miaoued loudly.

Lee's eyes opened.

'Oh, Hosanna,' she said. The cat slid off the bed, stretched and made his way to the door where he settled and waited expectantly.

'I think he wants to go to the loo,' said Philippa.

'Hosanna sees Gabriel,' said Lee.

'Oh, Lee,' said Philippa, 'What are we going to do with you?' She stood up and opened the door for Hosanna to leave, turned and sat down by Lee on the bed. 'What are we going to do with you, Lee?'

'Somewhere,' Lee said, 'I don't know where – in Africa, I think – there dwell two tribes, close to one another – I mean I think their assumed boundaries could well be adjacent – who hold diametrically opposed attitudes to the birth of twins. One of the tribes, you see, thinks of twins as special, precious, a good omen, a sign of approval, a gift from the gods. The other tribe, however, finds twins fearful, appalling, degrading, an aberration, because you see only animals have litters of young and therefore twins are considered to be inferior, a threat, so much so, in fact, that this latter tribe ritually murders them at birth. So, you see, the one tribe worships and the other tribe slaughters twins.'

Philippa looked round at Conrad.

'I don't see what that has got to do with anything,' she said.

'I know what she means,' Conrad said.

'What do I mean?' said Lee.

'You mean that you can believe or not believe, that there's a positive and negative side to everything, that

83

it depends on how you look at it, that you can honour and accept or despise and reject. Ghosts, I mean, in this context.'

'Oh, I see,' said Philippa.

Conrad laughed and tried to tuck his shirt back into his waistband. 'Blast this fat,' he said. 'Has your ghost got a weight problem, Lee?'

'Can't you understand that he's as real to me as those twins?'

'Can you see it now?' Philippa, whose face was normally as radiant and untroubled as a child's, had not stopped frowning since Lee had started talking to her that afternoon and it annoyed Conrad to see it. He was troubled by thoughts of innocence and the loss of it when he dealt with Philippa, and knew that she feared his seeming decay. Damn Lee, he thought. And I've got the show to do. Doesn't she realize the effect that she is having on other people?

'You do realize the effect that this is having on us?' he said.

But Lee was too absorbed.

'Do you know,' she said, 'I have never seen him in this room. Oh, I see: he's leaving me free to dream. He visits elsewhere but he leaves me my dreaming space. Space to dream. My own inner spirits. I see.'

'Lee, get out of this house.'

'You sound frightened, Conrad. Big baby.' She was, astonishingly, smiling.

'I am frightened. No, I'm not frightened, I'm para-lysed, like a jellied eel. I like my ghosts behind the footlights, darling. Crazy ghosts, complicated ghosts with fake faces and a lot of verbal. I mean, does he speak, this apparition? What am I saying? I don't believe a word of this. Get out of this house, Lee. Go away somewhere for a while. What does he want, this geezer? God, you know what I think? I think that

84

you've got house-itis. It's a common disease. People do leave something of themselves behind in the houses they've lived in, the Japanese recognize that in some way, I don't know how. I think that previous inhabitants are sacred, like household gods. You screwed that beautiful ape and now you can't get rid of him, that's all. It's like a nagging wife. I like the greasepaint, heart, can't cope with light waves.'

'You think I'm mad, neurotic.'

'No, I don't think you're mad – '

'Lee.' Philippa laid the palm of her hand on Lee's forehead. 'You're boiling. You were icy a while back. You're ill. What about these dreams? Your father, you mentioned your father. You never talk about your mother. This is you, you know. You're here, not Gabriel. This is about you. I think Conrad's right. It's rare but it can happen. Shut up, Conrad. I don't know about ghosts. It sounds like something time-warpish, feverish, not dangerous, weird, maybe true, but I don't think it matters. It's you. You're in some kind of spiritual trouble. It doesn't matter whether Gabriel is here or not, really. It's you. You need you back again. Then even if he is here you won't see him because you won't need to see him, if you see what I mean. Conrad's right – go away. From Gabriel. From the household spirits. From the Lee-in-this-house-Lee. There must be something, oh, you know, unresolved. Something in you unresolved. Go and sit on a mountain.'

Lee took Philippa's hand from her face and held it to her mouth, then placed it down on the bedcover.

'No,' she murmured. 'No, I won't go and sit on a mountain. I'll go home. I'll go to where my home was. I'll go to London. I'll go to my mother's house. I miss my forebears. The funerals happened within three months and then I came down here. You're right. There's a hole in me. Maybe if I go and fill it up, Gabriel will go away. Or my eyes won't catch him. He'll still be here but I'll be whole. Bless you. Will you look after Hosanna? He'll be cross, but I'll go. Thank you. Bless you. I'll go.'

'Well, hooray for Philippa.' Conrad was beaming benevolently. 'She's worked her magic.'

Philippa laughed.

'You see, darling Lee,' she said, 'you've brought us together, Conrad and me. Now never mind ghosts and all that malarkey. What we have here is a bloody miracle.'

'I've got to sleep,' said Lee. 'I do love you both so much. But I've got to sleep. And thank you. Bless you. I'll go.' She turned from them on to her side. 'I'll go.'

VI

A stocky blonde, hair short and spiked, sat on a large embroidered bean-bag with her hands around her knees and her eyes cast upwards and to her left. She didn't reveal what she was feeling, she just looked rather caught and aggressive. A long, thin brunette sat on another bean-bag very close to her, staring down at a focus somewhere near the edge of the blonde's left thigh. The brunette seemed full of feeling. Her face looked anguished as if she had been secretly angry and victimized for a very long time and it was just beginning to seep out. Her face threatened a volcano. Behind the brunette there stood a man whom Lee had seen in a long-running television serial, playing a detective. He was gazing forwards and he looked as if he had just stepped on a drawing-pin. The bean-bags caught the eye really, Lee thought. They looked enormous and magnetic and were brilliantly adorned.

The brakes of a bus screeched and Lee jumped. She turned away from the theatre photograph and stared, hostile, at the bus in the way an elderly person will crossly confront a jutting paving-stone on which he has stubbed his toe. Conflicts on the stage, she thought. As if we haven't got enough in real life. Oh.

The scaffolding had startled her. She had thought the department store that stood opposite the theatre unassailable in its pale-green elegance. She had not seen the building for three years and the projecting, metal construction offended her as impetigo would, sprouting from the face of a beautiful woman. Three men stood, tiny, at the very top of the geometrical iron web, leaning their arms on its highest horizontal bar. Their heads were the size of flies and moved to and fro as they presumably spoke to one another. Even grand buildings seem frail when you're no longer a child, Lee thought. You learn that the buildings are frail, people are passing, and doctors are presumptuous. She remembered shopping with her father in that shop for a twenty-first birthday present. The elegance of his own style, the willingness of the assistants, the feeling that an endless flow of joy emanated from this eccentric and astute little man, the jade-green charm of the suit that was eventually chosen, the reserve, the luxury, the civilization of that day came back to her now as she stood gazing at iron scaffolding, aware of drunks in the square opposite and the depression that had undermined the world, and her, since the buoyancy of that radiant and particular day. Then she thought of Rokeya.

'R. Hunt', the label underneath the white bell-button said, in green-typed letters on a brown paper background. Lee felt a little puffed; the apartment was at the very top of a tall riverside block without a lift. The walls were maroon and the carpet was purple and the effect was expensive, but Lee felt as depressed as if she had found herself in the smelly hallway of a neglected and deprived residence. She debated whether to sit down on the carpet for a while but shook herself and rang the bell. Terror suddenly hit her like an iron arrow in the breastbone and her throat seized up and she choked. Demons and monsters, she thought. There's a folk-tale about some villagers terrorized by a monster on the top of a mountain . . . She heard feet shuffling towards the door from within, then a scraping of metal as if there were a safety device being used even though it was the middle of the day. Then three-quarters of Rokeya's olive-shaded face appeared bearing the same expression of suffering as it had all the years Lee had known her, relieved only by the same amethyst earrings and necklace of variegated amethyst chunks.

'No,' Rokeya said.

'Rokeya, please don't shut the door.' Lee felt as if she were fighting for her life. 'I understand why you need to. At least I think I do. But please, I just want to talk to you for a little while. Just to sort things out a little bit. Otherwise it's as if there's a monster on the mountain, no, as if some dark being haunts us both. Ghosts must be laid, Rokeya. Oh, please let's be civilized. Let's care. Let's be human. Otherwise the dark forces win, don't you see? Do you want us both to be haunted forever by the past? Do you, Rokeya?'

'No,' repeated Rokeya, but the door was still held open by an inch.

'Rokeya, I only want to talk. Silence speaks loudly and frighteningly like a ghost. Rokeya . . . I dream about him. I never wanted to hurt you, it was all in your mind. Neither did he. He was just . . . autonomous. Ghosts can disturb and destroy the living, Rokeya; please let me in. For five minutes? Five minutes of your time and patience could alter – oh, the universe – for me.'

Rokeya moaned.

'Oh, Rokeya, don't be silly. You always reacted as if you had had a leg amputated when people are just . . . oh, really. Five minutes is nothing to ask. Nothing at all. Really, Rokeya.'

Lee's briskness had been a last stand and she was ready to turn and walk down the five flights of stairs again when the door in front of her suddenly swung open and Lee found herself walking through the doorway. Aladdin's cave or Hades, she wondered? Oh, Gabriel, will I ever rest again? Will I ever find peace such as I found in your arms again?

Rokeya's flat was so precisely as Lee remembered it that she felt as if no time had passed between the last time she had been inside it and the present day. In a way time has not passed, she realized. In a way I am just as much here then as I am here now. Oh, Gabriel.

Rokeya's small living-room seemed, as it always had done, over-powered, infested, adorned, camouflaged, complicated and prettied by maddeningly elusive antique objects. These objects seemed to Lee, now as then, to be growing out of the environment, blossoming uglily, like strange new plants emerging from a darkened tree-trunk. A tiny, round, mahogany dining-table stood by the window at the far end of the room snatching cold, white light from the space outside. On this table Lee could see boxes, lots and lots of boxes, several brown square and oblong boxes, some imprinted with glass pieces, some engraved, some painted in blues and yellows, one octagonal maroon velvet box with a sliver of white silk escaping from its lid, two tiny onyx boxes and one large black box that looked to Lee like a coffin. Pandora's boxes, thought Lee. I wonder where she eats? I remember she and Daddy . . . stop it.

She could feel Rokeya standing behind her by the doorway still, exerting power. She sat carefully in a bucket chair, on a dark-blue satin cushion embroidered with a yellow dragon, and looked up at the mantelpiece.

'I like your jade vase, Rokeya,' she said.

'Say what you came to say and go,' she heard. She felt again that same deep chill, that same sense of horror she had always felt when in the presence of such venom, as if she were discovering that evil really did exist, that liberal attitudes were vaporous, that filth could find its way into the universe and be embodied and spread relentlessly, terrifying those it infected. Stop it, she thought, it's illness: there's something awry here, that's all – only influenza spreads. Pray, hold on, keep going, work. There's hope.

'Rokeya, I'm trying . . .'

Suddenly Rokeya was standing in front of her, looking down at her.

'Oh, please don't look at me like that, Rokeya, I feel as if you are trying to poison me.'

'You're paranoid, you always were. Laurence's friends told me – you were like it when you were a little girl, seeing things that weren't there, making up stories. You're paranoid.'

'Please, Rokeya . . .'

'It's you, not me. You've always tried to make out that I was wrong and you were right. But it's you there's something wrong with, not me.'

'Rokeya, there's nothing wrong with either of us, there's something wrong with both of us, please . . .'

'You can't hurt me. I've been . . .'

'I'm not trying to hurt you. You could never understand that. I want to heal, if anything.'

Lee suddenly heard a violent crack from outside the room, which was simultaneously thrown into stark relief by pure, blinding light. Rokeya looked like a figure in a strangely exposed photograph, silhouetted, caught, highly defined by the light, like a prisoner running from a concentration camp, cruelly and horribly revealed by a roof-top guard's spotlight. There was a vicious clattering as the rain hit the window-panes. The room had become a grotto savaged by a storm, inhabited by a monster, its walls and floor and ceiling

91

punctuated with distorted stalactites and oddly coloured fungi and treacherous moss. Then, as suddenly, it was over. The light returned to normal, the rain stopped and Lee saw that Rokeya was weeping.

'Oh, go, go, go, just go,' she moaned. 'Thirty years we had. Thirty years. You say you dream of him: I can't even have that. He's gone. "It's time you went," I said as I watched him go but I didn't mean it. He was in such pain. He loved me. I loved him. He loved me and I loved him, and you never loved anybody except yourself.'

Lee felt faint. It was so like before. The midnight telephone calls, the endless pleas – for what, she had never known – the suicide threats, the constant secret visits to reassure, to keep the peace for his sake, for her father's sake, for his sake only. She realized now that she loathed distortion, that she would never lay this ghost because this ghost was real, this ghost was her and this ghost was forever.

'He's gone,' Lee said. 'You're still here. I dream of him, my father. Death should change things, but nothing changes here. I'm tired, Rokeya. I'm so tired of trying to reconcile things and people. I want to live with the living. Please try to understand: I'm so tired of living with the dead.'

'Are you all right, miss?'

Lee was cold suddenly as if she were sitting in a seawind.

'Wait, Rokeya,' she said.

She opened her eyes and saw a river, its surface shaking beneath the icy draught, the ducks bobbing slightly as they followed one another, seeking sanctuary.

'Can I help in any way?'

A young policeman stood over her to her right. The wind seemed to be coming from her left, bitter in the sunshine. Her body jerked and she sucked in her breath as if she had suddenly received a painful blow.

'Are you ill in some way?' The policeman's face was oddly pretty under its helmet, sweet and full of concern. Lee felt a wave of self-pity in response, so that she had to brace herself with pride.

'Oh, no,' she said.

'You were talking to yourself, love, and, well, sitting all alone and with your eyes closed. I just thought . . .' His expression was so tender that it shocked Lee. No lover ever looked at me so tenderly, she thought.

'No, it's all right. I walked here from across the river, and I must have overdone it. I was asleep. I must have been dreaming. It's all right. Thank you.'

'Oh. Well. As long as you're all right.'

Lee watched the policeman's back as he walked away from her and saw Rokeya, her crimson lipstick smeared down over her chin, her navy robe ruffled and gold-trimmed, her eyes watering involuntarily. Then she just saw the policeman's back, getting smaller.

The power of these people, she thought. They re-form themselves anywhere they choose to haunt me. Where's my strength? Where's my youth? Why did I come here? I came to London to lay ghosts, not to conjure them up. She saw an empty sandwich packet on the wooden bench beside her and remembered that she had decided to eat lunch in St James' Park. But I was running, she thought. Running. This is not the place.

Seated in the tube train, she felt as if she were thundering through the earth in a time-capsule, guided by a power greater than herself, without real roots or destination. She found herself concentrating too fiercely on the face of a girl opposite her, as if to ascertain the reality of her fellow traveller. The girl was very beautiful. Her eyes, her nose and her mouth were all round and definite and soft, and her hair surrounded her head like a designer's hat, Afro-styled and aggressive. Her dark-brown skin picked up the deadening light inside the train and reflected it strangely so that her face looked almost silver. She caught Lee's eye and Lee felt an electric shock pass through her. I'm too highly strung, she thought: I must contain myself, not stare. Perhaps Philippa was right? Perhaps Gabriel is not really there? Perhaps I just see things, make things up? Perhaps I'm not quite sane? And yet I know. I'm sure I . . .

The train pulled in at her station and Lee got herself out into the street, touching too many people, climbing ugly grey stairs, looking at posters advertising Tampax, warning about Aids, promising relief in the Bahamas, selling newspapers, selling theatre tickets, selling life, she thought, but it can't be bought, not really, it's within.

The men had disappeared from the top of the scaffolding when she emerged into the street again. They must be at lunch, she thought. Nobody says hello to you in London, I'm too naked here, the air is bare, nothing meshes. I must complete my business here and go home.

When she found the street she wanted she stood and waited before walking down it. A drunk sat on the step of the pub on the corner, his head in his hands. He lifted it and looked at her, and she saw that his skin was like a Red Indian's, incredibly weathered, his eyes red-raw, his mouth cruel, damaged. He looks like the brick wall he's reached, she thought, and walked by. The houses of this street, the street of her adolescence, the street of her father, the street of the rich, were elegant and preserved by comparison, daintily adorned, graciously windowed, almost scented with

94

wealth. This is an imposition, she thought. I am impor-
tunate. I dare not do this.

She reached the house in which her father had lived
and saw that the door was not quite closed. She walked
up the wide, white steps and gently pushed it open.

'Mrs Ridley?' she called into the hallway. 'Mrs
Ridley?' She pushed open the door a little wider and
stepped inside. The hallway was as she remembered it.
The large dark hall-piece stood there to her left with the
tenants' letters sitting on it. The wallpaper was the
same pale-green and the carpet beige, thick, respectable. She could see the kitchen through an opened door
at the end of the hall and the two doors leading into
Mrs Ridley's part of the house on her right.

'Mrs Ridley?'

The further of the two doors opened and an elderly
woman came out, using a stick.

'Who's that?' she said. She had dark glasses on.

'It's Lee, Mrs Ridley, do you remember? Laurence's
daughter. I'm so sorry if I'm disturbing you. I've only
popped in for a few minutes. It's Lee.'

The woman stood in the hallway for a moment like a
blind person unsure of her direction.

'Lee,' she said. 'Come in. I can't see, I've had a
cataract operation. Come in, Lee.'

She turned and went into the room again with Lee
following her. She's a grey figure by comparison, Lee
thought, muted where she had been abrasive, with-
drawn when she had been a firebrand. A ghost of a
person, thought Lee. Stop it. It's me, I only see ghosts
now.

Mrs Ridley settled herself in a green velvet armchair,
laying her stick carefully on the floor beside her. She
sat with her back to the window and Lee felt somewhat
at a loss faced, at last, by the elderly woman in the
opaque, black-lensed spectacles and the expensive,

95

rather drab suit, framed by sun-rays admitted through the tall crimson-curtained opening. Mrs Ridley, however, came straight to the point.

'Now, tell me, my dear, did you get your little inheritance?'

I need not have worried, thought Lee. Time doesn't alter attitudes and facts. She knows and remembers, this grand old lady. She's on my side. She sat down on the heavily bolstered arm of a brocade chair opposite her hostess. A much-needed calmness filled her. She was still accepted here.

'Yes, I did,' she replied, gently and politely. 'I bought a house by the sea with it. It makes all the difference, really.'

'What on earth possessed you to go down to the sea?' asked Mrs Ridley.

Lee was startled by the almost aggressive note in Mrs Ridley's question and had to remind herself that old people do not like change, do not like precipitate action, especially from those they have become used to. I mustn't bristle, she thought. I must be loving.

'Well, property is so much cheaper down there and I've always liked it and, well, there was such a hangover. It all left such a hangover.'

Sitting outside my childhood home, waiting for my mother to come home, even though I had watched her die, she thought. Looking for my father, even after his cremation, in the coffee bar where I used to meet him. Fearing Rokeya's poison. Facing the concerned but meaningless expressions of those not bereaved. Wondering why on earth they were not all friends. Blaming myself for not bringing them together. During the storm there were moments of joy and light; the aftermath contained only the sickness.

'It leaves a hell of a hangover,' said Mrs Ridley, and Lee felt relieved as if she had been ashamed of her

96

suffering and had had it authenticated at last. 'I'm so glad you came to see me. One doesn't know whether to telephone or what. I didn't know what to do.'

I'm doing the right thing, thought Lee. This is peace-bringing. I am gathering threads together and the cloth is becoming its pattern.

'Rokeya died shortly afterwards, you know.'

There must be a cloud passing over the sun, Lee thought. The room has gone dull. Strange – I didn't notice any clouds. There was that wind, of course. She can't have said that. She can't.

'Oh, did she?' she responded.

'Yes, she did. She died in a nursing home somewhere in Earl's Court, or Putney, I'm not quite sure. I saw it in *The Times*. It would be interesting to know what she did with all the money he left her.'

If she's dead then I am free of her, thought Lee.

'Yes, it would,' she replied, 'although I suppose it's nothing to do with me really.'

'I should have thought that it had a hell of a lot to do with you.'

'She got rather hysterical,' Lee said. 'They were all potty towards the end, weren't they? Batty?'

'Completely batty.'

Don't let me down, Lee heard her father shouting. You don't care, she heard Rokeya moaning. Don't kid yourself, she heard the doctor threatening. Then my Rokeya was a ghost, she suddenly thought.

'This was about eighteen months ago that she died,' Mrs Ridley went on. 'In a nursing home.'

Then whom or what have I been seeing, Mrs Ridley?

'Well,' she said aloud, 'she didn't last long, did she?'

'No, she didn't last long.' There was a knock at the door. 'I have to be getting along now, Lee, that's the damp man and I'm going to leave him here while I go to visit a dear friend round the corner. I can't see. I've

97

had a cataract operation. I'm going on eighty-two now, you know.'

'I'm so glad that you're still up and at it,' said Lee.

'Oh, yes. Of course, I've only got this house now. You may say, well, you're lucky to have it, but . . .'

'Oh, no, I think a bit of property makes all the difference.'

'Yes. Come along, my dear. You will phone me, won't you?'

A short tubby man was waiting at the front door in grey overalls, beaming.

'Hello, George,' said Mrs Ridley. 'Do you remember Mr Pembroke? This is his daughter.'

'Hello,' said the man. 'Yes. I do remember.'

'Hello, George,' said Lee. 'He was a nice chap, my Dad.'

'A very nice man,' said George, and Lee could not be quite sure whether he remembered or not.

'Can you give me a lift, George?' asked Mrs Ridley.

'Of course, Mrs Ridley,' he replied.

And then they were in the car.

And then they were gone.

The sun was blazing. There was no wind. There was no past. There were no clouds. Lee stood, stranded, cut off from the future. It all looks so different to me, she thought. Perhaps I'm waking up. Just one more hurdle: there's still Rose. There's still Rose to visit. Just one more trip over one more river. A little further south and I'll be free. Just one more dive down. Three miles south and fifty miles to the sea and . . . home?

A woman with hair the colour of the purplest of peacock feathers was singing on a yard-high rostrum. Along the front of the rostrum there was painted, in large, white letters, the phrase 'SWIPE ME'. Lee sat with her hand gripped tightly around the curved handle of a pint mug of beer and tried to work out who could have decorated the rostrum with this masochistic phrase and when and why and what it meant to the writer and whether the evening's entertainment was aware of the invitation signalling beneath her feet.

'*There's a small hotel* . . .' 'Patricia' sang into the microphone with her eyebrows trying to reach her hairline and her free hand symbolically gathering the audience into the chorus. A green lurex dress shifted itself up and down her scraggy body according to the dictates of her arm movements, and her face looked to Lee like a Restoration comedy mask, the only possible reason for the thickness and high colour of its make-up being the pockmarks underneath. Her audience consisted of five punk kids at one table and an elderly couple at another who both sat staring, not at the singer, but straight ahead of them, a half-pint mug in front of each. The beige-gold colour of the liquid in the glasses reminded Lee of Hosanna's coat when he appeared dull to her, real. When she was tired. The only other person in the bar was a tramp who sat without a drink, muttering imprecations and occasionally turning and flashing his bloodshot eyes in the direction of some imaginary enemy to his right and stabbing the air with one crooked finger. Lee wondered why the barman tolerated him but when she looked towards the bar she saw that the barman seemed hypnotized by the antics of the pub's female singer, not pleasantly, but as if he had been created permanently attached to a painful but essentially dependable puzzle. There was a pool of liquid on the floor near Lee that looked like urine. She felt as heavy as the smell of beer in the air, as crude as the wood of the tables, as cheap as the picture mirrors on the walls.

'Oh, Rose,' she said silently, 'you make my heart

want to burst out of me. How could you have wasted your life in such places? You with your gipsy beauty, you with your trouper's guts, you with your generous and violent love?'

'It's all I've got in life,' her mother replied, with that wide and tolerant, devious and undefeatable smile that had enslaved Lee when she was a child. 'You'll understand when you get a little older.'

Lee swam underwater in a warm and dark and all-embracing ocean.

'But I am older, Mamma. Can't you see?'

Rose turned her dark head to look at Lee, chuckling.

'Why so you are. Why, you tower over me. I am so proud of you, darling. I would give my life for you.'

'You drink too much, Mum.'

'I've always had a drink, love. When your sister died it was all I had to hold on to. You can't take that away from people.' Her face, with its Roman beauty, twisted up suddenly, hostile. 'I don't care what you think of me, Lee. I don't care what you think of me. Don't get morbid about me. I've had my life. Now you enjoy yours.'

'We played cribbage together by an open fire during the long winter evenings in our room.'

'That's the past.'

'Then you drank till you fell over.'

'That was my privilege.'

'Oh, Rose, come back to me. Tell me you haven't disappeared for ever. You went from me when you drank. Tell me you haven't gone from me now that you are dead.'

'You've got to let go of me, darling. I was tired of the struggle. It was the same with my mother. Your father wouldn't let me go to her when she was dying, but he couldn't come between us. I knew the moment that she went, I felt it. I had to let go of her, I had to. This is not good, what you are doing, calling me back like this. We go when we are ready. Let go, Lee. Let me go. I waited until you came to me in the hospital, I had to. And then I went. You must let me rest. I know what is happening in your home. You always had something . . . extra . . . something I could not get to. Something I could not understand . . .'

'What do you know, Mamma, what do you know? Please. You're the only one who can help me, you always were. It's too cruel if you are gone. God is not like that. You know, don't you? What do you know, Mamma? If you would just tell me, just tell me what you know. Then I'll let go. Please, Mamma, tell me.'

Suddenly Lee saw the exhaustion in the folds of skin beneath her mother's eyes. The indentations in the flesh of her cheeks looked like inroads carved by tears.

'I don't know, love. You've got to find your own way. Let me rest. You were always so powerful. I was at a loss with you being so beautiful and intelligent and all that. You've got to find your own answers.'

'But you were beautiful too, Mamma . . .'

'No. Leave. I gave you your life, not me. Let go of me, Lee. See now, you've made me cry. You're lonely, Lee, I can feel it, despite all your friends, your ghosts.'

'Mamma, what do you know about my ghosts?'

'No.'

'Mamma . . .'

'No.'

Lee laughed.

'You lead me on, Mamma, and then you run away. Same as always.'

A giant wave broke, somewhere high above. It was a signal, Lee knew.

'Another drink, madam? You can't sit here laughing like this, you know. You're in a public house.'

'Mamma,' Lee screamed, but the breathing had

101

stopped, the frown on her mother's naked face had cleared away. The pink tubes feeding her nose became redundant as the heart stopped pumping, Rose's blood left her face, and Lee herself started gasping for breath. Panting as she fought against the fact of death, panting as she integrated shock, panting as she realized a need to re-enter Rose's body, to deny her own life, to dissolve back into the embryo past, the womb, to disappear, to hand herself over once more to her mother, to die too, anything to stay with her, anything but this, anything but individuality, anything but alone-ness, anything but a self without a mother, anything but Rose's death.

'Don't touch me, you fucking bastard,' she shrieked, as the barman reached out to touch her arm. 'Don't touch me, don't come near me, don't even look at me, you bastard. You're not fit to kiss the ground they walked on.' She sounded to herself like a working-class heroine of a '50s black-and-white film, one of those who suddenly, to the bafflement of steady spouses sometimes played by people like Max Bygraves, and to the consternation of concerned mothers, frantically and uncontrollably asserts her rights. The triteness and immaturity of her own words and attitudes embar-rassed Lee but she could not withhold what streamed out. 'I don't know what is happening,' she thought. 'This scream is like the body of a burning aeroplane crackling, cracking. But I don't really know what is going on. I'm lost.'

'I wouldn't address me like that, madam. You're disturbing my customers. If you're going to get bolshie I shall have to ask you to leave. I'm sorry about this. You seem like a respectable sort of a lady, really, but I can't have people laughing like that and screaming and abusing in my pub. Now, if you're not going to order

102

another drink quietly then I think it would be best if you went on your way.'

Lee realized that there was no longer a sound of singing in the bar and when she looked up saw 'Patricia' staring down at her. She was standing at the front edge of the stage with the microphone hanging from one limp hand by the outside of her right thigh. The drunk was still raving and the elderly couple still seemed transfixed, but the punks were focused on her, their expressions fearful, and Lee saw that she, while gone, had made a noise, stopped things, alarmed them.

'Oh, I'm so sorry,' she said, 'I'm afraid I've been working too hard.'

'We're all working, madam,' said the barman.

'Leave her alone, Jack. Go and get a good night's sleep, love,' 'Patricia' urged, sounding honest for the first time that evening.

Lee wondered whether these strangers remembered her mother. She wanted to tell them about her, to share her ghosts with them, to beg from them some mutual memory, some working-class wisdom.

She knocked her knee painfully against the corner of the table as she stood.

'I'm so very sorry,' she said. 'So sorry to have disturbed you. I shan't be back anyway. Not now. I live a long way away, actually. So silly. Goodbye.'

Let me not be mad, she thought, in the street outside the public house. They think I'm mad. 'Gone' is the word they use. Conrad and Philippa don't believe me, not really. I'm hitting my head repeatedly against something that isn't there and I suppose that that could be a definition of insanity. I remember sunshine in the morning, I remember when a relationship enhanced reality, I remember when friendship meant faith. I remember good learning and running gags and reasonable ambition. I remember a certain belief in the unchangeability of certain things. And when God took those things away from me? When God thrust the abhorrent upon me? Did I not have the spiritual strength? Was that when I went mad? Was that when I started seeing ghosts? Was that when I started losing contact with the living in order to research untold-of matters with the dead?

The railings of the public lavatories on this side of the river were dark-green, heavy and ancient. The streets were filthy. The department store on the opposite corner was a giant, baroque box holding mass produced objects of a profound and miserable neutrality. Let nobody near me assert, thought Lee, that sickness strikes identically against rich and poor alike. You drank because you were poverty-stricken, Mamma, both in pocket and in spirit. You were unwell because nothing outside of you encouraged you towards health. What is making me ill? What are these unwelcome products of my psyche? What is real? Gabriel 1? Gabriel 2? My dreams? The lodger? Mamma, Rokeya, my father, me? The past, the present? London, the sea? Conrad and Philippa think they are real, and their reality gives them the right to doubt mine. Will you be there when I get home, Gabriel? Has this exorcism washed you away as well? Or are there degrees of ghosthood just as there are degrees of warmth and sanity and beauty and livingness and dyingness?

The land was scattered with stars. Mischievously winding strips of darkness were bordered by throbbing globules of orange light. The moon was full and round and pale and spoke of duplicity and peacefulness. The train-carriage that Lee sat in was empty. The outskirts of her home town excited her as a magical cavern will a child. I have died, she thought, and this is heaven.

Structures are settled, electricity enlivens, apertures astonish. There are no people left, no ghosts. I am alone. I feel tension in my left hand, my left cheek, and a pain beneath my shoulder-blade. I throb. I live in my body and things outside are separate. I love only Hosanna.

What now?

Issues.

What now?

Ghosts?

Here is the station.

What now?

Gremlins?

Somewhere there is love.

And now here is the steep, steep hill.

Climb, snail, climb.

Fear.

Still there?

What now?

Hosanna.

Fear.

Fear.

Fear.

Grainy, pale wood of front door.

Strange how insecure keys always make me feel.

Brilliantly created keyhole.

What now?

Gabriel?

Open, open, open.

Fear.

Houses are never empty.

What now?

Light.

A small, silver model of a cat. That jet-handled letter-opener from Whitby. Poems on the wall. A new stain on the carpet. Damp.

What now?

Spaghetti in long, glass jar.

Who lives in this house, I wonder?

The universe is stable. We rock it.

Hard draught from under cellar door.

Grip the floor with the toes. Monkey always in me.

Cat.

Cat?

Fear.

Frown.

Ghosts can't steal.

Where?

Oh, my love.

Warm snout.

White belly.

Silly.

Sneaky.

Hiding.

Home.

'Hello, my darling. Hello, my sweet. So warm. Hello. Moulting, is it? And fatter too. Such adventures I've had. Hello, soft lump.'

Hosanna.

VII

Larry clicked a pair of castanets he had found in Lee's attic above his fair head and stamped his feet on the kitchen floor and flung his head back.

'Tara. Tara. Tara,' he crooned. 'Mr Drinkwater's got a drink problem and young Emily's sleeping with the lodger and Mrs Kay expects her three-year-old to counsel her. Tara. Tara. Tara. Joanna's got a tumour and another terminal disease and is threatened with repossession and Mr McGinity is in an iron lung and can't pay his electricity bill. Tara. Tara. Tara. Tony Smith's a bigamist and his wife doesn't like it and Miranda's on the game and claiming. Mrs Thatcher doesn't care and Katie's pregnant and alone, ravishing Reagan's over there and I'm working my fingers to the bone. Tara. The rich get richer and the poor get poorer, my accountant's on the fiddle and I'm an overdrawer. Mrs Hardy's . . .'

'Stop, stop, stop, stop, stop, Larry. I'm trying to make a banana cake.'

'Mrs Hardy's gone bananas and all the asylums are full . . .'

'No, no, no, you must stop. I can't bear it. It'll turn out like a blancmange. Oh, please stop. It's too tragic.'

Lee was laughing and peeling bananas and feeling cross and wondering about a dream wherein a frowning angel laid gentle hands on her while young people with long black hair and bizarre head-dresses danced around her. 'Go and play somewhere else,' she pleaded.

'Patronizing, she's patronizing me. Just because she owns the house I'm living in, she thinks she can patronize me. I go out and tend to the suffering populace and she sits at home and patronizes me. It's disgusting. Disgusting, I call it. Life's not fair.'

'Life's perfectly fair, Larry. I'm just trying to make a banana cake. Why shouldn't I? How can you be so silly. Why, I can remember . . .'

'Oh, no, she's going to tell me about the time when she arrived at King's Cross station, pregnant, with a wage-packet in her pocket and no home.'

'No, I'm not. Go away. You're too silly.'

Larry gave up and left the room and threw himself on to an armchair in the living-room. He stared at the empty television screen, at a loss, silenced. He's like a gazelle, Lee thought, that once ran free and now finds itself all tied up in an unregulated zoo. I worry for him. Blast, these bananas are too hard. I have my spirits to confront and he has his realities. I am continually rattled by his insecurity. I can't feel anything substantial in him, anything well-founded about him. Perhaps he'll have to go? No, too cruel. But am I strong enough to watch him trying to fly over things and skim around things and fritter energy and search? He still needs the freedom of a four-year-old, to explore, to laugh suddenly in surprise at the world, to be open, to wander with the secure knowledge of a base to return home to. These ghosts of mine are trying to reveal something to me, but he, I fear, will be cut off from himself, sullied, put down completely by all the conflict at earth level, the materialism, the panic, the meanness, the blocked souls, the rubbish. Oh, Larry, be a poet. Go home. Don't let them get you. Don't let them steal your essence. Don't bother to help them. Don't make people your chain and money your God. Live, Larry, live; just fly.

'Larry,' she said, 'I've just burnt my hand on the oven grid because of you.'

'That's right, blame the poor old social worker. God, that's a second-degree burn unless I'm very much mistaken. Poultice? Ointment? Cold water? Doc? Why because of me? Shut the oven door. Right.'

'You distracted me with your ravings. I worry about you.'

'You let people get to you too much, Lee. You're not a survivor. You need protecting from yourself.'

'I was thinking the same about you.'

'That burn.'

'It's best left alone. The air will cure it.'

'I've got to go.'

'Nobody's keeping you.'

'You're too aggressive, Lee.'

'Too this, too that: what's wrong with me? Why are you wronging me?'

'Oh, I don't know. You always seem so – I don't know – I can't imagine you nervous, about real things. You seem so . . .'

'What?'

'Out of it. Dizzy. In a rarefied atmosphere. On another plane. I don't know.'

'Go.'

'Bye, Lee. Take care of that burn. Bye.'

The phone rang.

'Lee?' The voice sounded scattered as if the sound-particles were being separated and deflected by raindrops.

'Who's this?'

'It's Meg.'

'Meg. I'm delighted. It's been so long. How are you?'

'Not well.'

A bird thumped against the front window of the house. It seemed to stay stuck to the glass, its shape twisted up, for a very long time. Then it fell. Lee remembered when a sparrow had flown in through the window of her bedroom when she was a child. The wallpaper of the room had been the palest of yellow decorated with tiny Japanese ladies in pink and grey kimonos. The bird had been a monster to Lee. She had lain in her child's bed and become aware of the reality of her heart for the first time as its beat quickened in response to the sparrow's wild meanderings. The bird had thudded against the wallpaper and started to flop downwards and then swooped round and up, seeming ignorant of the opening through which it had entered. It will come over here in a minute, Lee had thought, and thump into the bed. Then it will wing itself up a bit and fall on to me. It will fall on to my face and start to grip me with its claws and pound my cheeks with its wings. It is ruining my pretty room. It is something evil from the forest. It will kill me. I hate it. She had screamed so that her mother came.

'Meg,' she said into the telephone, 'a bird has just hit my front window. I should go and see if it is all right.'

'Lee, do you remember Philip?'

'Philip? Oh, yes. That party. Looks Slavic or something. Different.'

'Lee, we started an affair. I'm suffering so. He used to take drugs. For seven weeks since we fell in love, he hasn't taken anything. I thought that he had found his salvation with me. I thought that we were going to be able to love without fear. I thought we would be safe.'

'What happened?'

'Oh, Lee, I went completely mad. It was like one's worst fantasy. I went to see him in his house. I have a key. We trust – trusted – one another. I pray for him. I

110

love him. He was in bed with another woman. I saw him. There was a narrow, black skirt with a slit in it hanging over his chair. It's a sort of tapestry chair. I went bananas. Oh, Lee, you're the gentlest person I know. I hate to burden you with this. Lee, I'm heartbroken – isn't it awful? I was the Christian, I gave of myself completely. Oh, Lee, how could he? All I can think is, I was wrong in the first place. I was wrong in the first place. I was wrong in the first place.'

'It's sinister,' Lee said. 'It's sinister the way he's swinging between salvation and dissolution. You'd be well out of it.'

'I was lonely. You are marvellous. You say things just the way I sense them and can't say them. But what am I going to do?'

'Let go of him.'

'I can't. I love him.'

'Conquer your fear of cranes.'

'What?'

'At least you fear what's there. At least what upsets you is tangible. I'm not sure that what's bothering me is there at all, really.'

'What?'

'Listen. I'm a wise woman writing in a woman's magazine. You need a stronger sense of your own worth. What happens to you when you see a crane? Or when you find Philip in bed with someone else? What happens to the you that is still, after all, you?'

'I don't know.'

'Yes, you do. Sort of.'

'I fragment. I disintegrate.'

'No, you don't. You're a tower of strength. You see it's not cranes, it's not Philip, it's you. You don't believe in yourself. Nobody, nothing in this world can affect you if you know, really know, who you are. You've

111

given me an idea. I'm going to get a job as a problem-page goddess. Oh, Meg, I see ghosts. How can I get to grips with what is, almost undoubtedly, not there at all?'

'You've given me an idea, Lee. I'm going to go into therapy. I think there's a connection between the cranes and this thing with Philip. It's probably something to do with my father. We were never *close*, you know. I never even saw his penis. Why are you laughing? Never mind, you're a love. Thank you. I'll call. Bye.'

When Lee turned out of the door and looked down to where the battered bird would have landed there was nothing to see but the same old Z-shaped crack in the hard, grey pavingstone and a streak of blood. She was reminded, penetratingly, of swastikas.

Conrad took a black pawn and threatened the rook. Then he moved the black rook so that it sat solidly behind the white bishop, attacking it in response despite the presence of the white queen three squares behind the bishop. He was listening to Mahler and the emotions the composer always aroused in him were affecting his game of computer chess, making it turbulent, unconsidered.

'*Merde*,' he shouted, as the lights of the computer blinked interminably. 'I'm brighter than you, you bastard. Come on.'

He sat barefoot on an orange Japanese futon and occasionally contemplated the enlarged and deformed toe on his right foot with relish.

'I'm coming, I'm coming,' he shouted to the phone. 'Got you, you arrogant castle. Got you with Beau Knight. Hello.'

'Conrad, it's Lee.'

'Hello, Lee. Hear the bonhomie? Is the bonhomie coming across?'

'It would fill a Greek amphitheatre, Conrad.'

A snipe. She's well again, Conrad thought.

'You're OK,' he said. 'I can hear it.'

'I'm OK. Travelled back and around a bit. I saw some strange things. I'll dine you soon. No, not anything supernatural. You were right. Emanation of a neurotically disturbed mind. Succumbing to the power of another. It was a gremlin. Thank you.'

'Dine me soon. I'm an actor without a stage now.'

'I will. Goodbye. I love you.'

'I love you too, Lee. Ta ta. Don't let the bastards grind you down. Say boo back.'

'I will. Bye.'

The needle had caught on the Mahler record. Conrad used the back of his hand to knock the half-played chess game off the low glass table. The white queen rolled under the table and was not found for several weeks.

'I'm alone,' he thundered at the television screen. 'She's there, yet she's not there. She was with me, now she's not. Or is she? Where's my ghost? If only I had a ghost. Nobody knows anything. God help us. Shit.'

Lee watched Gabriel as he stood at the window facing out. His back looked comically enormous framed by the floral white lace of the curtains. This is a film trailer, she thought, and at any moment he is going to turn around and reveal himself as the hero, the hunted spy or the detective. Then the credits. He looks like Orson Welles in *Citizen Kane*. I don't remember this bit. It's out of character for him to gaze contemplatively out of windows. Will he turn? Can he see me? Usually it's just a short clip, one attitude, an advertisement only. Tantalizing. If your goal is non-fulfilment, get haunted. I dare not move.

The phone rang.

'Hello. Oh, Philippa. Yes. Yes, of course I'm all right. You're what? You're pregnant. Who by? No, I don't remember Giorgio. I'm not very good at real people. Phil, I'm so pleased. I hope you stay yourself. I don't know what I mean by that. Yes, I am all right. No, there's nothing here. There's no one here but me. I must have been overtired, Philippa. Some kind of hangover, probably. No, no more ghosts. Come round. Not right now but . . . I'll knit, no I won't, I'll crochet. Hooray, Phil, I'm happy. No, I promise you, I'm all right now. No mysteries, no freak appearances, no ghosts. Your baby must have frightened off the intruder. Sure. Tomorrow. Sure. Love to you both. Bye.'

When she turned she saw that Gabriel had settled in the armchair in the half-light that always bedevilled the centre of the room. His right elbow was leaning on the arm of the chair and his wide forehead was resting in his right hand as if he were suffering from migraine, troubles, fatigue. Again Lee felt as if she were watching something new.

'What's the matter, Gabriel?' she said. 'This isn't like you. You're a fighter. I don't remember this bit. What is it? Gabriel?'

The knocking on the door shook her like an earthquake. The apparition seemed to disperse into a million pieces and disappear like a killer wave in a storm.

'I want to talk to you,' Gabriel said.

Lee fainted.

*

114

When she woke she found herself lying on her bed. The curtains had not been pulled and the light felt harsh to her. The bed dipped heavily to the right of her where Gabriel sat, holding her hand. Her face seemed puffy to her as if tears had been drenching it while she had been unconscious. She felt as if she were not really there, as if she had not really been there for a long time. She tried to survey Gabriel's face the way an in-depth photographer would, with ruthless clarity. She could see each individual hole made by each tough, dark hair that helped to form Gabriel's thrusting chin-stubble. I am a romantic turned social-realist, she thought. Too grand. I need glasses. But I can see he's the worse for wear, the weathering the worker wreaks on himself. I can see that extra line on his forehead. I can see the way his eyeballs are unusually distended. I can feel how large and hard and dry his hand is round my damp and childish one. I am aware of the solidity of his bones.

'I've been seeing you,' she said.

'I've been seeing you, too,' Gabriel said. 'Up here.' He touched his temple with his right forefinger and Lee saw again the white scar across his knuckles, a remnant of pain from his childhood, still yelling. I pushed it through a window, he'd told her. I couldn't get through to them. Lone Gabriel. Gabriel alone. Gabriel the lonely.

She reached out her hand and touched the scar.

'No,' she said, 'I've been seeing you here. In the house. You never left.'

'Still trying to drive me mad?'

'Gabriel?'

'Yes?'

'Do you believe in ghosts?'

The mattress shifted under Lee as he stood. She watched him as he walked round the bed to the window and looked out. The time was shady, things settling, flowers closing, downbeat. She crept out of the day, back, down again into peace. A Christmas Day evening, a fire fading, flickering, golden wrappings, a snoozing baby, love. Family that once was. Oh, Gabriel.

He ran his fingers, tool-like things, through stubborn hair.

'I believe in what I can see,' he replied. 'I believe in what I can hear. I believe in you. I love you. I love you because you're real. I shall always love you.'

'But we exist on many planes, Gabriel.'

He turned and looked down at her. His eyes were cut off from any outside flow, angry, as if two parts of his mind were fighting.

'No,' he said. 'You drive me mad. You're there, I'm here. I love you.'

'Gabriel, you were here. Caught in time and space waves. I saw you.'

'I don't understand what you are doing to me. Let me into your bed again. Feel me.'

'Pull the curtains.'

When he was naked Lee lifted the duvet for him.

'I want to sculpt you,' she said.

'No,' he said. 'You drive me mad. Don't see me, feel me. Feel this. And this. Feel that. Let go. Flow. I love you. Let me in. I'm not caught in space and time waves. I'm inside you. Love me.'

She swam away and down to the ocean bed with him, laughing. She lived with him where there was no time, no space, no self. She touched beautiful, unknown entities in unexplored regions. She flew in water. She floated in air. She was lost.

'I'm going back to sea,' he said later.

'Ah,' she said.

'I can't be land-locked. I've spoken to someone, and they'll have me back. You talk of space and time: I

116

know only the difference between the sea and the land. I need it, love. I need the waves talking to me. I can't talk to people, they're too separate from me. I can talk to the waves. I know when the storms are coming. The waves are inside me.'

She screamed. She punched his face and kicked his legs and tore at his abdomen. She abused him and walked round the room. She abused him and sobbed apologies. He never looked away from her and she saw that the pain in his eyes had been his vision of the sea tearing at him, his soul screaming no, no to earth, no to this, no to her.

'I love you,' he repeated.

'The real you goes away, the unreal one stays here. Take your ghost with you if you must go. I hate you. I hate the you here and the other.'

He began to fear that she was really lost.

'There's a land me and a sea me, love. The land one doesn't work.'

'No,' she raged. 'You don't understand. Oh . . .'

'You're hurting yourself. Be calm.'

'Oh.'

The violence left her and she lay peacefully in his arms. She licked the scratches on his chest. She kissed his eyes. She smiled.

'Suddenly you're happy,' he said. 'Why?'

'Because suddenly I see.'

'See what?'

'That it's the other one that's important. I'm closer to the other one. I too cannot be earthbound. We're dominated by ego here, fraught with feeling. You sail away on the seas and I'll commune with my spirit. We shall both be released. I see.'

Later, they sat on the floor in the living-room and drank tea out of brown mugs. Gabriel looked wrong.

117

Wrong in this room. Wrong in any room. He's too big for air-spaces confined by walls, thought Lee. He's too rough for civilized structures. He's too full for the emptiness of routine.

'We love one another because we're freaks,' she said.

'I'm not a freak.'

'You look like Pop-eye.'

'Pop-eye is strong.'

'You're a funny mixture. A nice one.'

'I've never felt like this before. About a woman.'

'There are lots of women like me around that you would have felt like this about if you'd met them.'

'You're the one I love. Now.'

'Now that I know your ghost I don't even have to wait for you to come home from the sea.'

'Don't keep on talking about this ghost. There isn't any ghost. Things are real.'

'Do you think I'm mad?'

'No.'

'I don't know. I've always felt – dislocated. As if I was not really meant to be here. Maybe the ghost is where I am really meant to be. Somewhere else. Some time else.'

'I've got to work. Now.'

'Yes.'

'I've got to, love. You know.'

'Yes.'

I feel like an extension of him, Lee thought when he stood. Where does he come from? How does he get here? Why do I need him to stay here when he weakens me in the way an earthquake undermines a city? What flaw in me allows him to do this? *Where* does he get to in me?

'Goodbye,' she said. Maybe a miracle. He's so big. Too huge for the doorway. That's it. We've moved in through the looking-glass and now we're too big, too enormous for egress. He'll move to the door and be foxed. Trapped. I could trap him. He'd tear down the walls. He'd grow and grow until he burst the house apart. He'd thrust a window-sized fist through a window, he'd kick off the roof, he'd roar until the walls crumbled, he'd explode. I love you, Gabriel. Oh, Lord and love and light that flows through everything, give me the goodness, the strength. Stay here, my soul, don't go with him. I'm lost. Now the tears again. Now he's with me. Now his arms are around me. Now he's kissing my face. Now his face is wet. Now his hands are holding my head, holding me in, helping me not to fly away, apart, dissolve. Now I'm left again like a trapeze artist falling. Now we're apart. Now his back recedes from me. Now the vicious lock does its terrible work. Now things are moving over there in that engin-eered space between the inner and the outer. Now the door seems to move of its own accord. Now I hear the slam. Now he's gone.

Lee sat on the floor, holding her pain. An embalming, dramatizing, strait-jacketing, tearing, humiliating, rot-ting and sacred pain. I am a wounded panther, she thought. This is anger, then. This is an anger I have never known. It is devouring, fragmenting and vilifying me. If I run after him and shoot him, blow him away, destroy his body, annihilate, the pain will be released. God help me. I want to say something unutterable. Comically unutterable, for a nice girl like me. I want to say, 'One day God decided that he needed to crap and you, Gabriel, came into the world.' I want to tear him apart. I want revenge. And yet I know. I know. We bomb what we hate and the pieces of torn flesh become our constant companions. Oh, Lord, teach us how to forgive. Let me forgive, and I will love again. Only teach me to forgive. Give me one last chance, oh Lord, and I will forever approach the world with friendship.

119

Gabriel's ghost is gone. Gabriel has ousted it as a skyscraper will fragment a cloud, as a charging bull will shatter the morning mist, as a massive ink-stain will erase a delicate sketch. How did I encompass it, this other-worldly emanation? My father told me that when Darwin's *Beagle* appeared in their island channels, the Tierra del Fuegans did not even notice it because their imaginations could not grasp so vast a ship. You can read a person, you cannot read a person's ghost. It eludes you the way print must elude an illiterate. There's a pre-literate Gabriel and a post-literate Gabriel. We are tyrannized by verbiage and have lost our very soul. Oh, Gabriel. Go and live with the sea. Sail free. Love me. Just be.

With both hands she pulled her right foot out from under her left thigh and placed it flat on the green carpet as a dancer will consciously reorganize his body. With this foot and all the solidity and strength of her right leg she levered herself into a standing position. She felt surprised. Numb. But surprised to find herself materially connected to the universe again. You lead me to defy God and gravity, my Neptune, she thought, with your devilry and your mystical shadows, but they never leave me, not really, and everything else apart from their holding forces is false. Even you, Gabriel. Even you.

Her left leg almost crumpled under her as she walked into the kitchen. The pain as the blood flowed back into it made her laugh, it was so intolerable. She opened the white-painted door of the tall kitchen cupboard, and, reaching in, took out an old-fashioned mop, a mop with long, thick, grey, curling tendrils. As she closed the door she re-examined some cuttings she had pasted on it, jokes, cartoons, sayings, pasted on years ago, oh, years ago. One still made her laugh: 'Have you ever tried writing a play?' the little girl asked the dog who was typing on top of his kennel. 'Maybe you could be another "Shakespaw".' 'HA HA HA HA HA HA,' the little girl went in the next picture-square, and 'BONK' read the bubble as the typewriter hit her at the end of the joke.

'Gabriel is a virus,' she said aloud, holding the mop like a spear. 'More vital than I. Parts of us die that other parts may live. I must clean house.'

She leaned the mop against the kitchen wall. It looked like a drunken woman supporting herself against a building in the street. Then she went to the sink and filled it with lukewarm water and made the water frothy with soap-powder. She doused the mop with the bubbling water and moved the heavy tendrils over the kitchen floor until the pale-green surface was moist and dirt-free. She hoovered and swept, sprayed mirrors and wiped, dusted wood and washed walls. She gouged filth from the oven and melted stains from the fridge. She shook blankets and soaked towels and hung out rugs and cleared rubbish and freshened wardrobes. When she had finished she sat in the corner of her bedroom and wept. After a long time she looked at her bedside clock and saw that it was past midnight.

Hosanna, she thought.

'Hosanna,' she said. She hadn't seen him since Gabriel had come.

'Hosanna,' she shouted.

'Hosanna,' she cried out into the yard.

'Hosanna,' she whispered into the street.

'Hosanna,' she pleaded into the high cupboard that held linen.

'Hosanna,' she called. 'Hosanna.'

For an hour she searched. She looked for him in the oven, the fridge, the wicker basket that held waste-paper beside her desk. She looked up to the ceiling to find him, she looked in spaces too small to hold a bird.

'Hosanna,' she sobbed.

But the vacuum was ruthless and total. The house was clean. The house was empty. No dirt and no spirit. The house was as meaningless as outer space.

'Oh, Hosanna,' she surrendered, and held out her hands.

Hosanna had gone.

VIII

Demian's face was covered by a white, concave square of what looked to John like the netting used for bee-keeper's head-protection. The square was gently raised away from the face. John felt, not understanding, as if a virgin were taking off her knickers in front of him.

'Yes, that's him,' he said. The square was replaced. 'May I stay with him a while?' he requested.

There was nowhere to sit. Demian's body had been hidden, shrouded almost, by a deep-crimson velvet piece of cloth, edged with gold. He lay on the marble slab in the centre of the tiny oblong chapel like a king lying in state. An artificial pink rose had been placed on the red cover roughly in the centre of the body. A marble collage of celestial entities adorned the wall above Demian's head. In the centrepiece warped opalescent planet-images seemed to spill over gold, mechanical star-figures. On either side gold metal had been arranged on a wood background to create abstract angels, kneeling, praying, haloed but without faces, without radiance. Demian's body barely raised his pretentious camouflage away from the slab. He must have starved himself, John thought. Jesus.

When, later, he heard Larry's voice on Lee's telephone the tears seemed to flood his throat. If I speak something will break, he thought.

'Larry, Demian's killed himself,' he said. He rushed

in, then, with many words, many more words about awfulness and pills, and if onlys and sadness; words that were curses and words that made the issue opaque and words that sounded trivial because he was so angry. 'The bastard,' he said. Then more words about his own father who had taken his own life, then retracting words, self-hating words, words weaving webs around his own egotism, then words that made no sense to the listener, words he himself was unaware of uttering as the tears wiped out reason. He heard Larry asking why, and realized he had been deaf. I'm in shock, he thought. And waited. Larry asked why again.

'Larry,' he said, 'I don't know. You know what he was like. He got twisted like his arm. He couldn't recognize love. How can anyone live like that? But I don't know. He has no relatives, you know: I was the one they called on to identify him. He left this note. For me. But I don't understand it. Or maybe I'm too scared to – I don't know. It said: "I'm spiritually dead already. This act has as much relevance as treading on a dead beetle." Jesus, Larry. He believed he had no soul.'

'He was wrong,' Lee said when Larry told her. She was in the middle of wringing the water out of a red rayon skirt she had been washing at the kitchen sink. She let it fall back into the water when she heard what John had told Larry. 'I shouldn't have washed this skirt,' she said. 'It says so in the instructions. Now it's shrinking and the dye is coming out – look at the water, it's bright red – you see, you ignore good instructions in your wilfulness and laziness and pride and you pay for it with a ruined skirt. Yes, I did hear what you said. And he was wrong. Yes, I know you're upset. It must hit you and John terribly hard, being friends of his and so young and all. But I can't pretend; I feel nothing. I saw that he probably encountered his own body as

124

worthless and warped and that he identified his body as his self, but he was wrong. This was not what God was saying to him, it was what Demian was saying to himself. He was a fine person. He did have a spirit. He does have a spirit. He killed only his body, and, like the rest of us, his spirit is freed by his bodily demise. Our pain lies in our bodily selves, Larry, not in our souls. Demian's the lucky one at the moment, believe me. And don't get mixed up between his act, and the feelings you have as a result of his act. I know how you feel. Stay cool.'

'You'll be saying that he's still here next. That you can see his ghost.'

Lee felt a muscle spasm in her back. It over-pressurized a nerve in her spine and made her want to scream. She wiped her hands on the white T-shirt she was wearing, leaving pink smears all over it. Then she walked into the living-room and sat down in an arm-chair. Larry stayed in the kitchen for a while and then followed her.

'How did you know about that?' she asked him when he had reached her side.

'I overheard. The night you were with Conrad, in your room. I'm sorry. I was on the landing. It all came through the door.'

'And Philippa.'

'What?'

'Philippa was here too. You were eavesdropping.'

'No, Lee. Honestly. It came through the door. It arrested me. I admit that I could have walked away . . .'

'It's all right. But – you're too young.'

'Philippa's young, too.'

'I know. That worried me. But she's . . . spiritual.'

'And I'm earthy, I suppose. What are you laughing at?'

'Oh, Larry, nobody on this planet would call you

125

earthy. It's not your affair, Larry, that's all. It shouldn't be bothering you. Put me down as a nutter, do. That's all it is.'

'I've got to go, Lee. I've got to leave. It's not you – I hope you believe that. You're not a nutter: if you were it would be easy. I mean I could stay if you were, it wouldn't be too much for me. But this – there's something up, Lee, isn't there? I mean, there's always been something odd, here. I've felt it while pretending not to. I mean, this ghost thing I heard about, and now Demian. It's beyond me, Lee. I'm scared, that's the truth.'

'It's all right, Larry. Of course you must go. Actually, I agree with you: there's something awry here and I seem to be caught in the middle of it. As a matter of fact I think that I'll sell this house. So you've done me a favour, you see. You've probably saved me from some kind of demonic sacrifice. I'm joking, Larry. You move on, and thank you, and I'm sorry if you've been disturbed, and I'm sorry about Demian, and I shall shed the deceptively comforting skin of this house, and all will be well, Larry, you shall see, the estate agent will save the day in the end.'

They were saying too much. What are all these words? Lee thought. It's as if we are gabbling the end of a play we are in. We can't wait to leave this theatre, this atmosphere, this trap. We want to get into the street again, to shift into normality, to chat in the pub, to laugh again. Goodbye, Larry. You achieved more than you will ever realize. Gabriel and I saved you from falling into your own image, if you could only see. But you're too young. Shivering. A cygnet out of its waters. You're losing hope. And, yes, I am partially responsible for that. So go. Soft Larry. Fade out.

Farewell, Larry.

*

When contracts had been exchanged on the house Lee arranged to go and stay in Wales for a while with friends, a couple with a two-year-old boy, who lived self-sufficiently, an 'alternative lifestyle'. I need the break, Lee had thought. I've been beleaguered.

Gabriel had appeared no more in her house in any form. I have cut him off, she knew, as a doctor will cut off a much-needed limb to save a life. But no – for I am not a cripple, I have no debility, and something other than myself is doing this. She felt rigid like a telegraph pole, communicating perfectly, functioning flawlessly, but with no heart, no soul. I will not die from this, she thought. I will live. By the day before the completion of sale all the goods in her house had been gathered together in one room downstairs, some packed in wooden crates, some in black leather cases and tapestry bags, some still living free.

Where are you, Hosanna? she silently asked as she surveyed the accumulated props of her drama. There is no more fun in you, she said to her curvaceous African drum. There is no more joy in you, she said to the Cornwall-born painting of Hosanna. There is no more life in you, she said to the old-fashioned studio photograph of her mother.

It was a freak day. The sun was attacking England, and the temperature was in the eighties. When she had bought some food in the local grocer's that morning people had been excited. Everybody looked more open, a bit stunned, silly. For Lee everything was being spotlit and she was seeing the people around her as if for the first time. The grocer was talking ten to the dozen as he served his Mars bars, his detergent, his potatoes.

I must walk, she thought. Everything is ready. Ghosts only live in the dim light. There is no past.

There were hordes of people down by the sea-front.

127

It's like an exodus from a spoiled country, she marvelled. The sun was so matter-bleaching, so pure, so icy that the sea was almost invisible as if the heat and light had killed it. Only the people seemed distinct, each individual carved out in the lemon-whiteness like moving, high-definition sculptures. The noise was appalling, as when too many birds gather together in agitation. I must get out of this, she said aloud. She could have screamed and the sound would have been accepted as part of the cacophony. She realized how terrible the noises of war must be.

A mile along the beach she found relief. The visitors had not reached this far, preferring what was on offer in the town. There were vast, sun-reflecting gaps between her and the Regency-white mansions on her left and the insistently moving sea on her right. She turned away from the road and started treading her way through pebbles towards the ocean. She did not know what she was going to do. Somebody or something seemed to be trying to speak to her but she felt cut off like a prisoner in a sound-proof box. Fatigue hit her. She was a few yards from the sea's shifting edge. Her blood seemed to have turned into heavy oil in her body, and something was dragging her down so ruthlessly that she let herself fall into the harsh carpet of pebbles. She felt a pebble cut into her elbow. She heard a bus go by behind her. She saw birds whirling in the stark sky. A second before she slept she caught sight of a windsurfer falling in the far distance. How icy, she thought, how strange. Then she too felt herself falling.

She dreamt that she was searching for something glorious: it could have been money, it could have been love, she did not know. And in the end she found two things. Again, she did not know what they were. All she knew was that the one excluded the other and she could not have both. So she schemed until she found a way of having the second thing without losing the first. But she was not comfortable about this. A woman with red, radiant, curly hair came up to her in her misery and said: 'It's all right. The others, they will never know about this second thing. You will get away with it. You can have both.' Lee, however, dreaming Lee, did not trust this woman deep down, she felt that she might tell on her.

Then somebody gave her a square wooden camera, a perfect camera made of light-coloured wood and pine with a beautiful hollow in the middle for the light-rays to pass through. Dreaming Lee took to this camera immediately and held it delicately and lifted the front-flap and looked through it in order to focus on something and take a picture of it. She saw the smiling face of a beautiful young girl, a child almost. She did not know how to respond to the resilience of this smile, the brightness of the white-gold hair, the apple-red glow of the cheeks, the indestructibility of the expression. She realized that the child was smiling straight at her but she was too tired to engage with her, too detached to make contact, too hidden to do anything but take a photograph and her fingers felt too weak even to do this. She felt a tap on her left shoulder. When she turned her head she saw the calm face of a man, a gentle man, a debonair man, a wandering but caring man. His eyes were still as still pools for a moment as he looked and then suddenly became like spikes.

'You're thinking too deeply,' she said to him.

He looked at her, properly, again.

'Let's just be happy, shall we?' he said.

Simply. He said that. Simply that.

He quite simply said, let's be happy, Lee thought as she woke. According to her watch she had slept for about six minutes. Who speaks to me? she wondered. I feel as if I've been given knock-out drops. Who needs

129

to speak to me so urgently that they lie me down on myriads of pebbles by a sun-scorched sea in the southern part of England? *Let's be happy, shall we*? he said to me. Well. If I hold on to these things they go, and if I let go of them they go, and so my life goes.

She heard a large vehicle draw to a halt behind her on the main road. The noise was loud enough for her to swivel herself round, prop her chin on her hand and stare. The vehicle was a white coach with 'FOLLOWERS OF JESUS' painted in black lettering on its side. When the driver had opened the door there emerged a stream of African men and women, all barefoot, and all dressed in ankle-length, white, flowing robes. They all walked around to the back of the coach and waited for the driver to open the boot for them. Out of the boot they took crate after crate of apples, of pork pies, of oranges, of Pepsi-cola, of crisps. There seemed to be a leader, an enormously tall man with a long, heavy, gold chain round his neck who bore in front of him a large picture of somebody, framed in rough wood. The new arrivals trod their way over the pebbles behind this man carrying their crates and smiling as they approached the waves. They differ from the sun-holiday populace in some way other than their skin and their garb, Lee thought. Their body-beings are so strong, so formed, so resilient that you feel that everything, anything would just bounce off the surfaces of them and away. There are no edges, no dampness, no little crannies to collect rust or mould or germ. These are healthy people. As the sun strikes their heads it plays for a while, scatters silver seed and dances away again, unnoticed. The pebble beach is dirtier than they realize but when they stand up from it clinging shell-dust and subversive oil-slicks and persistent grime will fall away from their white robes, leaving them untouched, pristine, still-saintly.

People walking along the promenade were beginning to stop and lean on the iron bar at the top end of the beach to look at the Africans. Soon a fairly large crowd had gathered and men were holding their sons up so that they could stand on the bar to get a better view. The mood of the unexpected audience was open-minded, jolly, participatory. The crate-people took no notice of them but arranged their food to the left of them, erected a cross in front of them while their leader pulled an angled prop from behind the picture he was holding and positioned it in the pebbles to the right of the dedicated gathering. Then they all sat down in a fashion so orderly that the files they formed were almost identical and equidistant. They looked like perfectly planted flowers in a flowerbed.

And then they chanted.

At the first waves of other-worldly congregational sound Lee swung her body away from the sight of these people and curled herself into a womb-like position, hugging her waist with her arms. She felt as if everything wondrous in the universe had started to sing to her. The chanting rose in volume and fell, syncopated and flowed, loved and released, flew and dived, teased and reassured and elevated and entranced and redeemed. The chanting moved. The chanting universalized. The chanting existed. The chanting absolved self. Now I am free, Lee thought – but in the thinking of it I am no longer so. I lose self only to reclaim self. Oh, damn me. This nugget that I call 'I' would bullet its way in even on the music of the spheres. I am not lost and so I have lost. She curled herself round more tightly, torn now between her life and the Africans' voices, and slept.

Much later, it seemed, she awoke and when she turned over and looked towards where the chanting had come from the African men and women had eaten

131

and were packing away and decamping. Into the vacuum that the loss of her communion with these people left flooded, terrifyingly, all the impressions, events, images and words of the phase of her life just ending. I was not really there, she thought. I have been watching a film. Oh, God, I've seen this movie before, must I watch it all over again? Perhaps I am drowning. This schism. I must speak.

She saw that the leader of the religious group had separated himself from the majority and was standing near to the sea's edge and looking directly at the horizon. He stood straight like an elegant, modern building with his large, black hands gently hanging by his lower body. She felt attracted to him as to Jesus. I lust after this man, she thought. What is this trick that my body and my ego are playing on me now? The brashness had gone out of the sunlight, and the air had a chill. Her hero could have been transfixed in the light from the Trinity, she thought, but it was cold light, cold, cold light. She shivered, and got up, digging ridges into the hostile pebbles with her sandalled feet. I am singular, exposed, she said inwardly. I need him.

When she reached him he did not turn his head to acknowledge her. His profile looked as ancient as a Red Indian's and as young as a street-child's. She wanted to kiss him, to soften him, to diminish him in some way so that she felt safer, more human. But it was not what she had come to him to do. This yearning was misplaced, a smoke-screen, the devil's seductive work. I must speak, she thought again.

'I wonder,' she said to this man.

He turned to look at her then.

'Yes?' he said.

'I don't really have a religion,' she said.

'This is sad,' he replied, and she felt that he did not refer only to her remark.

'But,' she said, and waited. He had turned his head back to the ocean. She saw that his ribcage was moving almost violently within his robe and that the skin of his face was a little stained in some way. Perhaps he has wept, she thought.

'But,' she repeated. 'I have been seeing, I mean feeling, no, communing with, aware of, there are no words, the spirit of a person.'

He closed his eyes and she saw that the movement of his chest had stopped.

'I mean, when the person is not there. The person is not dead. The person is just not there. Yet he is.'

'You love this person.'

'My friends think that I am losing my mind. And I am wondering whether it is the Devil's work.'

'You love this person?'

'I'm just wondering. Is there anything . . . I feel so sure that you and your people here today know more, have a key, no, just know something more, than I, than us. I am wondering, I suppose, although I hate to sound impossibly naïve, whether there might be anything in your religion, in your beliefs, or your understanding of belief, that might help me with this, that might help me to come to terms with it? Words sound absurd. I'm sorry.'

'We mark the truth with words. We do not reveal it thereby. You are right. I – we – the spirit world is assumed where I am coming from. Life would not be life without it. It is your perplexity that is odd, not your spirit-person.'

'But do you really believe in ghosts? I'm sorry. I shouldn't be looking for confirmation, outside myself, I mean.'

'You love this person? This spirit of a person?'

'Oh, yes. Well, I did. We lived together for a while.'

'Sometimes there has been something left unsaid, a

gap unfilled, a breach. The lost one seeks – to speak, to remedy, to punish, sometimes.'

'Yes, but you're talking about the ghost of a dead person, aren't you? This man is alive. I'm sure that I can, could, see both him and his spirit-self. No, it's a ghost. Really. A plain, old ghost.'

Her mentor smiled, then frowned as if in great pain. She could not leave it. She wanted to tear out the truth, to demand it, to extract it with magnets of iron, to burn it out of this man with a desperate scream if needs be.

'Tell me,' she commanded. 'Do I really see him, this other him? No, I do see him – but am I, do you see, meant to see him? Tell me. Do you believe in ghosts? *Do – you – believe – in – ghosts*?'

He turned his face back to her and she shook as if with a sudden, electric shock. She had never before seen or felt such vitality. Something seemed to pour through his face and overwhelm her, something molten, timeless, glorious. I worship this man, she thought.

'It is not for me,' he said, 'to believe in anything.'

He reached out his hand and felt her forehead.

'You are sick,' he said. 'Soul-sick. It will take a long time.'

He lowered his hand and gazed out to sea again.

'It is not for me,' he repeated, 'to believe in anything. You know the truth: you are afraid of it, that is all. It is not for me or for you to believe in anything. It is only for us to accept what God in his mystery may send to us. I feel that if you do not continue to love then you will die in some way. But there, I presume. This may well be the man in me rather than the man of God.'

He gathered his robe up around his knees and smiled at her.

'Now I must leave you,' he said gently. 'My people, you see, are awaiting me.'

Indeed, when Lee looked inland she saw that his congregation were all inside their bus and only he was missing, the coach door left half-open to receive him. As she watched him striding up the beach she tried to consider what he had said but with his loss the full weight of her grief hit her with a thud that stopped her eyes, her ears, her brain. So I have lost it all, she thought, my childhood, my mother, my father, my home, my real Gabriel, my ghost Gabriel, my Hosanna, my past and my soul. This, this is the only reality, the deathly reality of loss. And now, oh, yes, I feel real. This, then, is my reality that no one other than me can inhabit; this is no movie. I have lost them all, and live like my bones, separate and ageing in a cleverly concealing skin. *'I feel that if you do not continue to love you will die in some way.'* Let me inscribe these words on this papyrus of a person that I have become and trust, my saviour, that one day they will enlighten me. In the meantime I must move in life, though not alive in it.

Heavy and hoping, Lee moved through air inland towards the building she was now to walk away from.

Epilogue

'Mummy, why have we come here?'

'I used to live here a long time ago, darling. Before you were born.'

'Yes, but why have we come here *now*? Does Daddy know we're here?'

'Don't you like it here? Don't you like the house?'

'No. The gates at the back door look horrible, all fally down.'

'It hasn't been looked after properly.'

'Mummy, you're holding my hand too tight.'

'I'm sorry, darling.'

'Mummy, can we go and see the sea? You said that we could see the sea. I don't like it here. It feels funny.'

'Oh, darling. Mummy used to love it here.'

'Why? Let's go to the sea, Mummy.'

'Oh, I had a boyfriend and we lived here. A long time before I met your father. There was a ghost.'

'What do you mean, a ghost? You're frightening me, Mummy. You look all funny. Come on, it's widgy here.'

'What's "widgy"?'

'"Widgy", you know, weird, funny.'

'Oh. It was pretty widgy then too.'

'What widgy? How widgy? Why widgy? Widgy, widgy, widgy.'

'Well, there was a person in the house who wasn't really there.'

'Don't be silly, Mummy.'

'You know, you and that Daddy of yours patronize me a great deal too much. Why am I silly?'

'Because, because, if there's a person in a house then the person is there.'

'Ah. That's what I thought.'

'Unless it's a ghost, of course. Ha, ha. Widgy.'

'I'm not sure that I believe in ghosts.'

'We're not ghosts, are we, Mummy?'

'Of course not, darling.'

'And Daddy's not a ghost?'

'Oh, no, for sure. Daddy, for sure, is not a ghost.'

'Then who's a ghost?'

'There was a man called Gabriel, darling. A nice man, but a rather strange and powerful man. I was a little bit silly about him. And – this is widgy – I used to think that I saw him when he wasn't really there.'

'That's not widgy, that's zizzaway.'

'What is "zizzaway"?'

'Oh, Mummy. Zizzaway is when something is so funny that you want to zizzaway from it.'

'Ah. Of course.'

That night in bed with Matthew, her husband, Lee dreamt that she, Matthew and Hannah, their child, were adrift on a raft in the middle of a yellow sea. Violent serpents emerged from time to time to try to snatch Hannah from them and they warded the serpents off with pieces of wood and savage words. Soon, too soon, they became tired and could no longer properly defend their child. A serpent, the colour of khaki shot with spasms of red, came too quickly for them and slithered its vicious body around the waist of their daughter and drew her inexorably from the deck of the raft into the endless ocean. Lee screamed, Matthew groaned, the sea churned.

Then suddenly there was Gabriel, rising from the waves like a resurrected god. Giant-like and blessed, glorious and free. Beautiful, mammoth arms tore the serpent and Hannah apart. Lee watched the evil serpent flying through the sky like a disorderly comet and wept over Hannah as Gabriel handed her her daughter. Gabriel was smiling at her. He seemed as big as the world and as small as nothing.

'Are you a ghost?' Lee said to him in her dream.

'Let's be happy, shall we?' he said.

'Oh, Gabriel,' she replied. 'We will be.'

Then he turned and disappeared into his home, the enveloping sea.

'We will be, dearest Gabriel. We will be happy. We will be,' she cried out amid the emptiness that he left behind him.

When she awoke she lifted herself up and, leaning her head on her right elbow, looked down at her sleeping husband. His skin had turned gold on a recent trip to Israel and she felt her stomach clench with excitement as she absorbed, yet again, the strength, the magnetism of his features. And one day of course, she thought, one day, Gabriel, when all this is over, one day, Gabriel, when I've come through to the other side, one day, eternal Gabriel, one day, my love, one day, my life, one day, of course, we will be.